# Struggles and Triumphs

Cynthia L. Simmons
2 Cor 2:14

CYNTHIA L. SIMMONS

# *Struggles and Triumphs*

## WOMEN IN HISTORY WHO OVERCAME

HISTORICAL FICTION

Pleasant Word (a division of WinePress Publishing, PO Box 428, Enumclaw, WA 98022) functions only as book publisher. As such, the ultimate design, content, editorial accuracy, and views expressed or implied in this work are those of the author.



ISBN 13: 978-1-4141-1121-6
ISBN 10: 1-4141-1121-5
Library of Congress Catalog Card Number: 2007907694

# Contents

Acknowledgments

I want to thank my writers' group, Christian Authors Guild, for all the teaching and guidance. In particular I must thank R.T. Byrum, Diana J. Baker, Susan Schulz, and Mike Anderson. My critique group valiantly helped me edit these stories, so thanks goes to Robert Graves, Judy Becker, Bonnie Grant, Brenda Ward, and Marcus Beavers.

Jennifer Evans encouraged me when I started to write, and without her help, I might have given up. My personal editor, Heather Corhan, deserves praise for helping me polish my work. Cec Murphey guided me through my early efforts at fiction. All five of my children, Charity, Joy, Paul, Daniel, and Caleb, cheered me on while I completed the project. My husband, Ray, believed in me and applauded my efforts from start to finish.

# Introduction

Women. Who and what are we? We bear children, breast-feed babies, manage households, drive carpools, discipline our kids, run errands, take responsibility, and operate successful businesses. Yet a certain vulnerability lies at the core of our nature. Our hormones can create havoc with our emotions, and we long for security and love. Often we wish to be prettier and thinner, as if that would satisfy our inner cravings.

On the other hand, men tend to have greater muscle mass because of their hormones. In the past men have raped, oppressed, abused, and at times, considered women nothing more than property. Today laws protect many of us, but women in past generations had less freedom and fewer choices.

Does Christianity impact the lives of women? In this book, I portray the lives of nine prominent women from history—many have faith, but several don't. I sketch the thoughts, fears, and expectations of each. Some come from the same family, or shared friendship, yet each faces her own challenges. You will watch them struggle with oppression, search for love, seek for revenge, face danger, long for acceptance, and grieve over death. Those who know Christ find their way through heartache with God's help and guidance. Once you have read each story, I think you will better understand that faith in Christ improves the lives of women. And you will long for a closer relationship with the Savior. For those who want to go deeper, I have included questions for thought and discussion at the end of this book.

# CHAPTER 1

## Royal Crisis

"Your Majesty! You must awake. Your Majesty, this paper is of great import. Please, Your Majesty!"

The queen opened her eyes and saw her maid's chubby face creased with anxiety. Mary Odell's light brown eyes had a gleam of fear, and her full lips wore a frown. She had parted the red velvet draperies around the queen's canopy bed and now stood by its heavily carved Corinthian columns.

"Good morning, Mary." The queen yawned, stretched her slender figure, and sat up, adjusting her black, silk nightdress. Even at thirty-four, she retained her youthful beauty. Her light brown hair, now in braids, had a touch of auburn, and her big, gray-green eyes set off her oval face and fair complexion. "It is a lovely morning."

Sun streamed through the tall, multi-paned window beside the bed. Its rays glittered over the gold candlesticks on the carved pedestal table at her bedside and on the gilded frame of Henry's portrait which hung on the wall across the room. In contrast, Mary, a commoner, wore a simple gray floor-length dress with long, narrow sleeves, and a white vest laced over her very full bust. A white cloth cap covered her graying hair.

Mary held up a rolled parchment. "Your Majesty, you must read this."

The queen yawned and snuggled back into the covers which smelled of her home-made lavender and rose potpourri. "I had a late night at court, Mary. It is much too early to read. You read it to me. You should be able to decipher most of the words." Kateryn, whose name was pronounced Katherine, had married Henry VIII of England three years before in 1543. As a devout Protestant, she believed that every person should be educated. She had a Bible study each day with her maids, where she also taught them to read.

"Oh, n-n-no, Madam. No, I cannot." She shook her head.

"Mary? This is unlike you." She cocked an eyebrow while reaching for the paper. "Here let me see. I shall show you some words you recognize."

After another yawn, she unrolled the parchment. Once she began to read, however, she gasped and threw a hand over her mouth.

Mary trembled. "Something is amiss. I knew it. Those long words, I just knew."

Her eyes on the paper, the queen did not answer, but the color drained from her face.

"Your Majesty?"

Kateryn looked at her sharply. "Where did you get this?"

Mary, a deep crease between her brows, pointed toward the door. "I found it in front of the door."

"Which door?"

Mary Odell pointed to the door that led to the hallway.

The queen, her face almost white, leaned toward her and put a hand on her arm. "When?"

"I-I-I do not recall. Ten minutes, maybe." Mary shrugged.

She released Mary and dashed to the window, where she examined the paper in the sunlight. "This *is* the king's signature."

"Madam, is this *quite* serious?" Mary clasped her hands together and tried to see Kateryn's face.

The queen put the paper on the pedestal table by her bed and crossed her arms. "Did you see anyone in the hallway?"

"No, Madam!"

She moved closer. "Are you sure you saw no one? Think!"

"No, Madam. The hall was empty." She shook her head. Her frown deepened. "Is this truly grave?"

"Yes!" Kateryn plunged into the bed and ducked under the covers. "I am ill!

"Ill?" Mary frowned.

"Yes, I am ill. Send word to my sister straight away!" Kateryn's sister, Lady Herbert, served as her lady-in-waiting.

"Oh, yes, Your Majesty!" Mary curtsied. "What should I tell her?"

"Tell her I must see her now!" She shivered in spite of the blankets on her bed.

"Would you like me to bring you—"

Kateryn turned her face away. "I require nothing. Please send someone to fetch Lady Herbert *now.*"

"I shall do so and return anon." Eyes widened in fear, Mary rushed from the room.

*I must face this.* Kateryn swallowed several times and reached for the paper with shaky hands. *This is a warrant for my arrest, and it has the king's signature. It is my fault. I should have been more careful in speaking with Henry on religion.*

Her mind went back to the conversation she had with the king a few days before.

She found the corpulent king in his audience room, where huge tapestries covered the walls. Dressed in an embroidered doublet with full sleeves adorned by gems, the king wore a heavy gold chain around his neck and a small hat of black velvet decorated with ostrich feathers and jewels. An enormous frown creased his square face. He sat on an engraved throne and had his left foot elevated on red velvet pillows with gold tassels. White bandages on his sore leg had brown spots where the ulcers had oozed. His bejeweled fingers massaged his knee.

"Kate! Dearest! Come and look at my leg," Henry said when she entered his chamber. "The pain is fierce."

She curtsied to the king and kissed his hand. Then she knelt to examine his bandage. "This needs changing. I will send for my medical supplies. My herbal preparations will ease the pain."

The king gave a growling sound in his throat. "Cursed leg! I can barely think for the pain."

Kateryn walked to the door, opened it, and spoke to the doorman outside. "I need my herbal medicines. Go to my rooms and speak to Mary Odell. She can locate them."

"Make haste, knave," the king said.

Kateryn stepped behind his chair. "Lean forward and I will fluff this pillow."

The king sat forward while she removed the squashed pillow from behind his back, fluffed it, and returned it.

"Confound it! My footmen ought to do that. They are all fools," he said. He looked up into her face. "Thank you, dear."

"Once I make you more comfortable, I will dance for you," she whispered in his ear while massaging his shoulders.

"Ah! Yes, that feels nice," he said. "I wish you could do something for my head. It hurts too."

She raised her eyebrows and cooed, "Dear Henry, I will make you feel better. Shall I massage your temples?"

"No! Attend to my crippled leg first," he said. "The footmen should have summoned you with greater haste. You have considerable skill with herbal cures."

"I am glad I please you, husband. Would you like something to drink while you wait?"

"No! Confound it. I want the pain to cease." He gritted his teeth.

Massaging his shoulders, she sang a tune softly into his ear. The king sighed and closed his eyes.

Kateryn heard a discreet knock on the door, and she went to answer. "Thank you!" Holding a basket with jars of her herbal preparations and bandages, she came toward the king.

"Those knaves arrived at last. Fix up my leg, wife." He pointed to his leg.

She knelt on the dark oak floorboards beside the king and unwound the bandages.

The king flinched. "Ouch! Go easy, woman. Are you trying to hurt me?"

"I apologize, sir. The drainage makes it hard to remove the bandages."

Once she had removed the bandages, she massaged herbal ointment into the king's ulcers. "How does that feel now?"

The king took a deep breath and released it slowly. "That is much improved."

*He seems calm and relaxed. I think I can talk about the church now.* Aloud she said. "I have been thinking about the church."

Henry, whose eyes were closed, grunted.

"The minister read several Scriptures this morning in chapel. Do you remember that passage where Jesus says, 'I am the way, the truth and the life. No one comes to the Father, but by me'?"

The king opened his eyes a little and nodded.

"In that verse Jesus claims to be the way to God, not the pope, not priests, not sacraments, not good works. Faith in Christ alone gives eternal life. This is the essence of the gospel. The people of England need to know the gospel. You have made some changes in the church, but I think you need to do more. Your subjects are often confused about the truth, and I think you should finish what you started."

The king sat up to watch her work. "Are you finished with my leg?"

"I have to wind the bandages around this spot, and then I will be done." She patted his leg and gave him a brilliant smile. "I have completed the job."

"Now, sing to me," he said. He closed his eyes and leaned back in the chair.

She took his hands in hers and sang a lively tune.

Henry opened his eyes and gazed at her. "You can go now."

Kateryn kissed his hand, picked up her basket, and curtsied.

As she opened the door, she heard him say, "Farewell, dear Kate."

A sound outside her door brought her thoughts to the present. *Are the soldiers coming already?* She lay still, waiting for the moment when they trooped into the room, but nothing happened. Trembling, she eased out of bed and tiptoed to the door, where she listened. After a few moments, she sighed and crawled back to bed.

*Usually the king lets me discuss religion. But that night, he did not. He was irritable and grumpy. I knew it, but I tried anyway. I felt comfortable, because he has been so sweet to me. But I am not safe. He will send me to the tower. He has already beheaded two wives. It is a habit with him.* Another shiver ran through her body as she pictured the austere Tower of London where the king kept his political prisoners.

She rose from the bed and grabbed a shawl from her huge oak wardrobe. Wrapping it around her black nightgown, she eased over to her chest and picked up a book bound in red velvet. *Henry let me publish these prayers. He does not hate me. These took me weeks to write, because I was so careful not to upset him. He knows I have Bible studies in my chambers, and I thought he liked it when I debated with him.*

Closing her eyes, she imagined an axe in the hand of an executioner. She swallowed hard and rubbed her throat. "God, I did not want to marry this man. He executed wives in the past. I am his sixth wife, and I am terrified. What should I do?" A sob escaped her lips and tears sprang to her eyes. Dropping the book, she leaped onto the bed and scurried under the covers.

Lady Herbert, formerly Anne Parr, knocked and then entered the room. Glancing around the room, she finally saw her sister huddled under the covers. "Sister?"

Kateryn uncovered her head. "Read that paper beside the bed. I am doomed."

Anne followed her sister's eyes and leaned over for the parchment. "What is this?"

Kateryn whimpered and sank under the covers again. Her chest felt tight, and her heart fluttered.

"Sister, are you sure this is authentic?"

Kateryn pulled away the bedclothes to speak. "I know Henry's signature. I have seen him write his name often enough."

Anne shook her sister. "We have to think, to plan."

Back under the covers again, Kateryn replied, "Shall we plan my funeral?"

"No, I refuse to lose all hope. Try to think with me. This is not like you."

"I am going to die."

Anne pulled the blankets away from her sister. "Did you say something to make the king angry? Has he been rude to you?"

Kateryn, who was curled into a ball, pulled the shawl over her head. "No, he has been very polite. But I think I know what I did."

"What?"

She uncovered her head and looked her sister in the eye." The last time I saw him, he was feeling poorly. I brought up the gospel and told him England needed to know the truth."

Anne grimaced. "Oh, Kateryn! You should be more discreet."

"We often have friendly debates about religion. That night he cut me off. But he did not scold me or say he was angry." She balled up the fringe on her shawl and squeezed until her fingers turned white.

Her sister's eyebrows flew up. "You mean he lets you debate with him about religion?"

"Yes, we have gotten into some serious talks."

Anne rolled her eyes. "And when he gets angry with you, he has you arrested."

Kateryn tightened her lips. "Yes, his mistresses receive better treatment. As a believer, I could never be a mistress."

Mary Odell's plump form appeared in the room. She was breathing hard, and her face was red as she curtsied. "I forgot the time. It is almost ten, and you will be late for dinner." The royals ate the biggest meal of the day at ten in the morning.

Kateryn covered her face with her hands. "I am unable to eat. I am indisposed. Tell the king my disease will be fatal."

"What?" Mary looked confused.

She sat up and grabbed Mary's arm. "Tell the king I am mortally ill."

"Sister, are you sure this document is real?" Anne said, narrowing her eyes. "I know the Catholics dislike you. They could have forged it."

Kateryn shook her head. "That is his signature. I would know it anywhere."

"Then where did you get this?" She held the document aloft. "You have no access to his documents."

Mary had been about to leave the room, but she turned and walked toward Anne. "I found it, Madam."

Anne's eyes got big. "Found it? Where?"

Mary pointed toward the door. "It was outside the door, on the floor."

"On the floor?" Anne gave her a sharp look. "Sister, does this seem odd?"

Kateryn, her face pale, pointed toward the document Anne held. "I know it is real. Yet, I have no idea how it got there."

Mary curtsied. "Unless you need me, I will go and inform the king's servants that you are ill."

The queen nodded. "You may go."

In silence, both ladies watched her leave.

Kateryn moaned and covered her face with her hands.

Anne stepped over to the bed and sat down. "Now, let's decide what to do."

Sobs broke anew from Kateryn's throat. She rolled over and buried her face in her pillow.

Dr. Thomas Wendy was forty-six years old. A heavy set man with graying hair and a pointed mustache, he had served as the king's physician for fifteen years. Now he towered over Kateryn's bed. His keen eye noted her pallor and the panicked look in her eye. "Your Majesty, the king expressed great concern about your health. He sent me to look after you."

"I don't think you can help me," Kateryn said. "I have annoyed my husband, and he has signed a warrant for my arrest."

The doctor's eyebrows went up. "Very true! How did you find out?"

She waved toward the door. "My maid found a copy of the warrant signed by the king."

His face brightened. "This is good! You have a friend amongst the courtiers."

Her mouth twisted into a frown. "I don't think a friend can help me now."

"Oh, but you will not be caught unawares. You can make amends."

She lowered her eyebrows and puckered her lips. "What do you suggest I do?"

He shrugged. "Apologize. Remember when Cranmer angered the king? He gave the king an apology, and the king spared his life.

The queen shrugged. "How can I apologize for my faith?"

The doctor crossed his arms. "Then this is about religion?"

"Oh, yes!"

"The king made a remark about you."

Her eyes flew open, and she sat up in bed. "Tell me what he said."

He narrowed his eyes. "Promise not to quote me."

The queen nodded.

"He said you fancied yourself a professor and would now lecture him."

She bit her lip. "I feared as much. Thank you for telling me."

"If you like, I can prescribe something to help you relax and sleep."

Kateryn shook her head. "No, but thanks."

Dr. Wendy bowed and left the room.

Anne, who had watched the interview, came toward the bed. Her eyes glowed. "Did you hear what he said? He had hope."

Kateryn slid back under the covers. Her face sagged, and she closed her eyes. "I am tired of the stress and frustration of being the king's wife. I must measure each word, gesture, and phrase. The Catholics hate me and say evil things about me. I wish I could escape. When I die, I will be with the Lord. Perhaps this is for the best."

Anne reached over and grabbed Kateryn's arm. "No, I do not want to hear you talk like this! You must resolve to take action."

At that moment, they heard a knock on the door, and Mary Odell entered with Catherine Willoughby, Duchess of Suffolk, who was one of the queen's closest friends. The duchess organized and participated in the queen's Bible studies. Her husband, the Duke of Suffolk, was close to the king.

Mary Odell curtsied and came toward the bed. The slender, brown-haired lady followed behind her, and she bowed to the queen. "Madam, the duchess asked to see you, and I thought she might be able to cheer you up."

The duchess stepped forward with a gracious smile on her pretty oval face. "Your Majesty, I heard you were feeling poorly. I wondered if I could help in any way."

The queen extended her hand and gave a weak smile. "Dear Cathy, thank you for coming."

"She is distraught," Anne said. "The king ordered her arrest."

"This is serious," the duchess said. "In your position, you have enormous influence to help publish Scriptures and devotionals for the English people. You can help those trying to spread the gospel. We must save your life. Please tell me what happened."

Kateryn told her story and displayed the warrant. As she spoke, she struggled to continue. Tears distorted her face, and sobs choked her words.

"May I sit down, Your Majesty?" the duchess asked.

Kateryn nodded.

The duchess sat and took both of the queen's hands in her own. "I would like to pray with you. May I?"

The queen sighed and nodded her tearstained face.

"Almighty Father, I praise you for your sovereign rule over the universe. I thank you for access to your throne through your Son, Jesus Christ. You are not dismayed or overwhelmed by our sorrow and anxiety, and you provide for us…when we cannot provide for ourselves—" Her voice broke in a sob.

In a moment, the queen threw herself into her friend's arms. The two noble ladies, locked in each other's arms, wept bitter tears together. At last, their crying subsided to sniffles and sighs.

In a stronger voice, the duchess prayed. "Father, give us a dispassionate coolness while we consider our choices. Scripture says if we acknowledge you, you will guide us. Do that for us now. Help us to save the queen's life so she can continue her fine work here in the palace. Amen."

"Thank you!" Kateryn said.

The duchess sighed and pursed her lips. "Now, let us consider. Dr. Wendy indicated the king might relent if you handled the situation properly. Is that correct?"

"Yes! But what can I do? I must not deny my faith. I believe with all my heart that faith in Jesus is the way to eternal life."

"No, you must not deny what you believe!" She folded her arms and frowned. "Did the king find any forbidden books in your possessions?"

The queen shook her head. "No, I removed all of them."

"I worried that after the Catholics burned your dear friend, Anne Askew, the king's inner circle would insist on a search."

Anne Askew had been a long-time friend of Kateryn. She had given copies of forbidden books to various ambassadors who had delivered them to the queen's court. The ladies had read and discussed their contents. Recently, the Catholic party had tortured Anne to get information about her activities. They suspected she supplied the queen with books, but Anne did not confess, even under severe torture. The courts, dominated by Catholics, found Anne guilty and condemned her to death. After extreme torture, they burned her at the stake.

Kateryn swept her hand across her brow. "My husband never gave permission for anyone to search—unless he kept it from me. I had no reason to fear. He has been so gracious and loving."

The duchess gazed at the queen with narrowed eyes. "Then tell me exactly what Dr. Wendy said."

"The king did not like the fact that I gave him instructions. The doctor said my husband thought I had become an expert of sorts."

"Ah, now there is something!" A smile blazed across Cathy's face. "A king, or a husband, would not like someone dictating to him—on any subject. You can apologize for that, without saying you don't believe the gospel."

Light leaped into Kateryn's eyes. "That is it! I can apologize for demanding that he do something. I do often discuss with him to keep his mind off his declining health. Part of me hopes that someday he will see the reasons to trust Christ. But I have never dictated to him like I did that day."

"Wives must be careful to consider the command in Scripture to be submissive. Encouraging our husbands is good. It is fine to influence them—like your religious discussions. Telling them what to do is overstepping our boundaries. I have done it too. But my husband is not king, and I didn't end up fearing for my life."

Anne sprang to her feet and said, "I will accompany you, sister. Shall we dress and go right away?"

The duchess glanced over to the window and pointed out the fading light. "You have been in bed all day, and it is growing late. I suggest you approach the king tomorrow, after getting some sleep. Today has been very trying for you."

"I like that idea," the queen said. She was smiling now. "Cathy, pray with me again."

The queen, her sister, and the duchess bowed their heads again and prayed.

The next day, Kateryn rose and knelt in prayer. "Almighty Father, guide me today. Give me favor in the eyes of the king." She bathed in milk, and after her maids patted her skin dry, she covered her body with sweet smelling herbs. *I must not displease the king today.*

She chose a red brocade dress with a square neck and tight bodice. The sleeves were narrow at the shoulder, but opened into a bell shape that folded backwards at the elbow to reveal ermine underneath. Her full skirt had a triangular opening that showed a silver embroidered underskirt. A matching headdress and a long, beaded gold belt completed her ensemble.

Just before the ten o'clock meal time, she entered the king's chamber with her sister, who gave her a nod of encouragement. Her breath came fast, and she could feel her heart galloping. "Good morning, Your Majesty!" she said.

The king smiled when he saw her enter. "Kateryn! Are you feeling better today?"

She stepped up to the king and kissed his hand. "I am much better, sir. My fear is that I have angered you, and I would like to apologize."

His eyebrows rose. "So, do you still insist I take measures to purify the English church?"

Kateryn bowed her head. "No, sir. I do not."

He puffed out his chest. "Would it not be wise to wave a Bible under my nose? I might need correcting on some point."

She met his eyes. "No, I think you are able to read it for yourself."

He leaned forward and pointed to her. "Ha! Should I have you ordained as the first lady minister and bow to your wishes?"

Shaking her head, she said, "No, sir. I do not claim to have any superior knowledge. I am most pleased to discuss religion with you in the evenings to distract your mind from your discomforts. But I have nothing to teach you."

He smiled. "You will not give me lessons?"

"No! I was too forward. I am sorry."

"Then, dear wife, I forgive you," he said. He held out his arms. "Come and sit in my lap."

Kateryn felt a sweet pang of joy radiate through her chest as she walked toward him. Lifting her skirt with care, she climbed into his lap, and he kissed her.

"Give me that velvet box on the chest," the king growled to one of his servants.

The servant trotted to the chest and placed the box in the king's hands.

"I am giving this to you, Kateryn," the king said. "I know how much you like red." He opened the box. Inside, a huge ruby ring glittered in the sunshine. "The ring was made for my finger, but I shall have it made to fit you."

"Thank you, sir!" She kissed his cheek and smiled. "This is exquisite."

He turned her face toward his and caressed her smooth cheek. "I like to see you smile. I see lights dancing in your pretty eyes."

The door flew open. "The Lord Chancellor and guards, Your Majesty!" Lord Wriothesly, Lord Chancellor, marched in the room. Six beefeaters, guards from the Tower of London, followed behind him. Dressed in red, they were armed with swords and spears.

The king raised his voice. "Rogues, scoundrels! All of you, leave me, now!"

"Sir? I am obeying your orders," the chancellor said. He waved a paper in the air. "You signed this paper, and I am doing as you requested."

The king gestured toward the door. "Leave me, and take your men."

The chancellor blinked several times and frowned. "But sir…"

"Enough, go now!"

Fear spread across the man's face, and he spoke to the guards. "Let's go."

Kateryn turned toward the king. "Those poor men were afraid."

"They came for you," the king said. "They cannot have you, my excellent wife. Come, I will escort you to dinner."

"Thank you, sir," she said. She looked up and saw her sister, who was smiling. *Praise be to Almighty God! I believe you put me here for a purpose. Now I can continue to help your people.*

## CHAPTER 2

# The Price of Freedom

*I could throw myself over the stone railing and end it all.* Duchess Louise shuddered as she thought of landing in the rushing water below her. She could picture the water cascading and dashing over the rocks in the Itz River. The same gushing turmoil raged in her soul.

"This book dispelled my doubts," she said. Her small hand caressed the smooth, green leather of the book that lay before her. "But the truth haunts me."

The spring breeze penetrated the thin fabric of her dress, and she shivered. She pulled her shawl more tightly around her shoulders, and her eyes scanned the rolling hills, as if hoping to find another solution to her dilemma.

"At least here I shall be at peace." She sat on the patio of Rosenau, a hunting lodge her husband had refurbished. Since the villa sat six miles from the city, she felt safe. He seldom came here this time of year.

Louise lived in a small territory in southern Germany. Born to the duke of a nearby province, she grew up during the Napoleonic wars. Her father, however, made peace with the French invader, and she never experienced war. Instead, she grew up in peaceful surroundings and immersed herself in medieval stories of chivalry. Even as an adult, she clung to her romantic nature. Her petite figure, winsome ways, and lovely features would make any nobleman protective. The gauzy pink and white empire dress she wore accentuated her fragile beauty. Light brown, wavy hair framed her oval face, and deep blue eyes set off her fair complexion. In spite of her delicate frame, she had an unquenchable zest for life. Yet since reading the book before her, bitterness and anger had forced her to action. Louise, Duchess of Coburg, demanded freedom from a tyrant—her husband.

A maid stepped out of the French doors onto the patio and curtsied. "Your Majesty, Lt. von Hanstein to see you."

Despite her dark mood, laughter almost gurgled up in the duchess's throat as she saw the April wind tousle the young soldier's sandy hair. *I do believe good men still exist, and here is one of them.*

Von Hanstein displayed honor in his every motion. Wearing a uniform of forest green, his six-foot frame stood erect. The gold buttons and medals on his jacket glittered in the German sunshine. He came toward her and dropped to one knee on the cobblestone patio. "You called for me, Your Majesty."

"Yes!" she said with a chuckle. "Please stand. I need…I must ask a favor."

The soldier stood but kept his eyes cast down. "Yes, milady?"

Louise looked him over with a smile of satisfaction and said, "You may look at me, you know."

For a moment he looked up, and she saw his green eyes. "Of course, Your Majesty!"

She sighed. *I* do *understand. I am your duchess.* For a moment she looked toward the valley, wishing for another answer. At last she said, "This request will seem odd."

"Oh, no Madam!" His face held no emotion.

"I must explain…my situation." She stood and picked up the book.

His face turned pale.

She cocked an eyebrow. "You have some knowledge of this?"

"My lady, the book—"

"Yes, you heard—the book my husband banned." She turned and dropped it back onto the table as if it burned her fingers. "Yet every noble family has a copy, and I see them look at me with pity in their faces."

His green eyes met hers, and she saw deep sorrow in them.

"Did you notice the girl's age?" Her whole body trembled. "The girl had barely left childhood—when my husband lured her away and forced himself on her."

The soldier shook his head, but he maintained his noble bearing. "Your Majesty...the story must be untrue."

A cry burst from her lips, and she bolted across the patio toward the stone railing.

In a moment the soldier saw her intent. He dashed to the railing, grabbed her around the waist, and pulled her to safety.

"You think I overreact?" Her blue eyes blazed into his pale face as he dropped his arms. "You trust the Duke because he parrots Luther's words? Words mean nothing. He intends to deceive."

"There is no possibility that the story is contrived?" Concern creased the soldier's entire face.

Her small body stiffened as she pointed toward the book on the stone table. "None! I recognize his actions, words, and techniques. He wooed *me* when I was a young maiden. Every attractive girl in Germany is in danger."

His face flushed in anger as he stepped back. "Your Majesty, how can I possibly help?"

She sank onto the stone bench beside the book and fingered the floral pattern of her empire dress. "Ernest was thirty-two when he came into my life. His dignified bearing and gallant words ensnared my heart. All my childhood I had read stories of heroic knights who risked their lives to protect their homes and their ladies. With his dark curls and fair skin, I believed Duke Ernest the noblest. At that time I knew nothing of men, but he excels at deception."

Von Hanstein watched her face with his lips pressed together.

With a sigh she crossed her arms and passed her hands over her dainty puffed sleeves. "An unsigned letter came to me, and its contents unnerved me. The writer made...disagreeable accusations. I shared the letter with my childhood playmate, but I feared telling my father. My father was a good man, but he demanded strict attention to behavior. I feared Father would accuse me of listening to gossip. And whenever the Duke came to visit me, his excellent manners and gentle kisses pushed away all my fears."

Von Hanstein coughed discreetly before he spoke up, "But Madam, surely your father..."

"You think my father also heard the rumors? I wonder. My father accepted him warmly, at first, but delayed our betrothal for months. I cannot say why father finally consented. If only I had Papa's advice now, but he has gone on to his rest." She ignored the tears that flowed down her face.

The soldier balled his hands into fists, and his face hardened.

A deep frown creased her brow as she pushed the book away from her and blotted her tears with the back of her hand. "After we married, I heard gossip, but I looked into his engaging chestnut eyes and refused to believe. Only after I had my second son did I see the outrageous flirting. Every pretty girl at court received his attentions—even in my presence. He behaved with such abandon—I would blush for him. Any comment about his behavior brought a rush of anger, and I learned to fear him."

The soldier's face now wore a dark frown, and he clenched his teeth.

"Recently, I made a slight reference to that detestable book...he grabbed my arm. He twisted until I cried out in agony. The bruises lasted ten days." She collapsed onto the stone bench and sank her head into her hands as sobs shook her body. After a moment of fierce crying, she paused. While dabbing at her face with a lace handkerchief, she shrugged and chuckled with a slight edge of hysteria. "I hate this feeling of helplessness."

The young man knelt before her and said, "I offer you my assistance."

"I knew you would listen," she said with a sigh. "My case is a sad one, but with your help, I might hope. I asked for a divorce. Ernest refused. My plan will not be easy, but I shall ask you to commit no crime."

The soldier bowed his head.

She clutched her small hands in her lap and gazed at them as the force of her grip turned them white. "I want to flirt with you at court. That is *all.* I hope to create a spectacle. If I embarrass my husband, he might then consent to divorce."

He raised his head, and she saw a flash of determination in his green eyes. "Yes, Madam!"

"I have seen you at court. What does your job entail?" She raised her eyebrows.

He nodded. "I am in charge of a battalion of men based at the Veste, and I manage the security at the castle in Coburg." The Veste, a fortress used in medieval times, had housed Luther during the Reformation. His brief stay there had given the small city prestige.

She pursed her lips a moment. "Ach! That explains why I have never seen you here at the Rosenau. Then I shall request your presence for any court event I must attend in town. I shall bring security matters to your attention. I only require you to treat me with cordial respect, nothing else. I simply could not do such without taking you into my confidence."

He bowed his head. "I understand, Your Majesty."

"Excuse me, Duchess, we are ready for you." The maid curtsied and motioned for Louise.

"Thank you, Letitia." Louise's face was pale, and she had dark circles under her eyes. She put aside her embroidery, rose, and followed her maid up the spiral staircase and into the bedroom. Trunks overflowing with clothing sat on the floor around the huge bed.

"We are almost ready to load the carriage," Letitia said as she pointed toward the trunks. "Is there anything else you require?"

With a sigh, Louise looked around the room. The cherry armoire, now empty—like her heart—gaped before her. She closed her eyes, swayed.

"Your Majesty?" Letitia said. "Your Majesty? Are you ill?"

Louise opened her eyes and looked into Letitia's brown eyes. "I saw the empty armoire, and it *feels* like my heart—empty. Last week I said goodbye to my two boys."

"Just sit down here, and I will get you some water." Letitia said as she motioned for the other maid.

"I am fine," Louise said, as she eased herself onto the simple straight chair beside the lush bedcovers.

Letitia accepted a glass from the maid. "Here, take a sip of some water."

"I must not sit. There is so much to be done," the duchess protested.

"You have lost so much weight that you are weak, Your Majesty," Letitia said, handing her the glass of water. "That dress you are wearing should be altered again."

The bodice of Louise's dress had a series of tiny tucks across the front, which should have fit snugly into her empire waist. Instead, the dress hung limply on her figure.

The other maid handed Letitia a damp rag which she now dabbed on Louise's face.

"I am a bit tired." Louise sipped the water and then closed her eyes.

"Ach, dear lady, you have been through so much." The maid patted her small white hand.

"Both my sons cried when I said good bye. They were so sick, and their little cheeks were so chalky." Louise's blue eyes filled with tears. "I shall *never* see them again."

"Madam, the doctor told me they had a simple childhood fever," Letitia said as she touched her mistress's arm. "They will soon be well."

"Yes, I know they will soon recover." A wan smile crossed her face for a moment. "I am tormented by the thought of losing them forever. God help me! I did not consider the price of freedom."

"Perhaps the duke will relent," Letitia said.

"Ernest? Relent? No!" Color surged into Louise's thin cheeks as her eyes flew open. "The man is evil, and now I can escape from him."

"He did make unthinkable accusations at the trial," Letitia said with a frown. "It made my stomach turn to hear his witnesses speak of you that way."

Louise shuddered. "He is guilty of much more, but *I* am pronounced the guilty one. Where is justice?"

"Ach, you must let your thoughts of the wretched trial fade," Letitia said with a frown. "If you want to live, you must get your strength back."

Louise winced and ran her tongue over her lips. "I hope someday I can *forget* my shame. Now I am an adulteress and a divorced woman. What could be worse?"

"The duchess needs some more water," Letitia said to the other maid. She accepted a glass.

Louise drank water from the glass and handed it back to Letitia. "Thank you! I should never have survived without you, dear Letitia."

"It is my pleasure to serve such a fine lady." Letitia raised her eyebrows. "I thought you would never succeed with the duke, but you prevailed."

"I stood my ground for an entire year before he gave in," Louise said as a weak smile spread across her face.

"That is good, my dear. Think of good things now!"

"I regret all this for von Hanstein too." Louise shook her head. "Ernest portrayed him as my lover."

"Ach, I should not worry about the Lieutenant." Letitia said with raised eyebrows. "He is a clever man who has friends."

"I must rise and prepare to leave." Louise sat up and straightened her floor-length skirt.

"But—"

The duchess stood and walked to the mirror over the dressing stand. "Perhaps a new hairstyle once we are settled. At least the courts could not touch Mama's property. I shall still have money." As part of the divorce, Duke Ernest took her father's lands, but her mother's property remained hers.

A maid named Alice, eyes wide with fear, burst into the room. Her face was pale and drawn. "M-M-Madam...there is a p-p-problem."

Louise frowned when she saw the maid. "Alice, what troubles you?"

The maid opened and closed her mouth while gesturing toward the front of the house. "The...men...they demand *you*."

She narrowed her blue eyes. "Men? Which men?"

"Men from the town," she whispered. Fear danced in her eyes. "You must come."

"The duchess is exhausted. Tell them she cannot come," Letitia said, hands on her hips.

Louise, a curious look on her face, brushed her concerns aside. "I feel fine now. I shall go."

She could feel the hair on her arms stand up and sweat run down her back as she followed the maid down the spiral staircase. Once downstairs, the maid led her to the handsome entrance hall. The huge oak door stood open to the September air, but a mob of men thronged the doorway. Their anxious faces peered into the darkened hallway. They wore homespun trousers and jackets. Some had beards, but all wore a look of determination. Many held rifles as well. With a gasp, Louise stepped back as they called out to her.

"Duchess!"

"Duchess Louise, come to the carriage."

"Duchess!"

"Your Majesty, we want to take you back."

"We would not hurt you, my lady."

She took a tentative step forward, and men fell to their knees.

Trembling, she forced a smile and looked at the throng of kneeling men. "Can I help you? Do you need something?"

The men slowly stood, and a murmur went through the crowd.

Her heart hammered against her ribs, but she kept a smile on her face, even though her cheeks felt frozen. "I see guns, and they make me fear you. What do you want?"

An older man with a full, gray beard spoke up, "You have no need to fear. You must return to Coburg. We will take you."

Another man from the middle of the group yelled, "Marriage is for life. We must reconcile you with the Duke."

A young boy from the right side yelled, "You belong to us, and we love you. We hope the Duke will see that."

She took a deep breath and said, "I need my trunks. Give me three strong men, without guns, to carry my bags down. "

Several men stepped up with hopeful looks on their faces.

She pointed toward three and waved them toward Alice. "Show them the way upstairs, Alice."

Letitia hovered in the doorway to help Louise don her woolen traveling cloak. Afterward, she turned back to the crowd, and the men parted ranks, making a path to the carriage.

"I want my maid, Letitia," she said looking back.

A bearded man with dark brown hair stood at the open door. "She must go in the wagon behind the men."

"Very well, I am ready." Nodding and smiling at the men, she walked forward. The dark-headed man offered a calloused hand at the carriage door. She put her small trembling hand into his, and he assisted her inside.

Once inside, she leaned back on the upholstered cushions and buried her face in her shaky hands. An odd sound made her peer outside, and she realized the men had unhooked the horses and were leading them away.

*Are they stealing the horses? No, the dark haired man is giving instructions. These men intend to pull me in the carriage rather than use horses.*

A male voice shouted. "Let's heave together now! Pull!"

As darkness fell, the carriage moved forward and then picked up speed. Out her window a sea of faces faded into the shadows. The murmur of their voices mingled with the sounds of their feet and the moans of the men who pulled. *Oh God, these men have guns. Please keep me safe. If they become angry, they might start shooting. They seem to believe in me. Is it possible that the people see what Duke Ernest really is?*

After what seemed like hours, the carriage came to a halt, and the men cheered. The door opened, and the dark haired man once more offered his hand. After she got out of the carriage, he took her by the arm. Flanked by two armed men, he led her to the ornate doorway of the Duke's Coburg palace.

Several armed men preceded him to the door and knocked. A servant, who held a lighted candelabrum, opened the door with a frown.

The armed men shouted, "We present the Duchess of Coburg! We present the Duchess of Coburg."

Louise stepped forward, and the man holding her arm released her as she walked toward the open door. At the door, the servant, wide-eyed, stepped aside to let her enter. The same three men came behind her with trunks and deposited them in the hallway.

In a hoarse tone, the servant asked, "Madam, where do you want your trunks?"

"Put them in the fourth guest room on the third floor."

He bowed. "Yes, Madam."

Still wearing her cloak, she walked up the steps to the Duke's receiving room. A maid entered behind her and lit candelabra that sat on the ornate furnishings.

"I never thought I would ever see this room again," she whispered as her eyes looked over the heavy framed paintings of her husband's family.

"Your Majesty?" Letitia entered the room.

"Yes, I am here." Louise turned and went toward her.

Letitia unfastened the hooks of Louise's cloak and stepped behind her to slip it off.

"Thank you, Letitia. What will happen now?"

"The men told me they are bringing the Duke here, too," Letitia whispered.

Louise gasped. "Oh, no!"

The maid leaned close and whispered, "They want to reunite you."

Louise collapsed into a French mahogany arm chair and put trembling hands over her face. "I thought I never had to see Ernest again."

"Hello, Louise," Ernest said, striding into the room with a look of disgust on his rugged face. "All of this is *your* fault. Coburg is about to riot, woman—because of you."

She rose and faced him, even though she trembled from head to foot. "What was I supposed to do, just ignore your escapades? I grew tired of your pious speeches about honor and your avid devotion to Luther's words. You have Coburg deceived, but not me."

Dark curls framed his angry face as he gazed back at her. She could see red-hot sparks in his brown eyes, and a vein throbbed in his temple. He strode toward her and twisted her arm behind her back. "Yes, you fool. Women should be blind and stupid. You tried to be smart. Fool!"

"Ouch! Let me go." Tears poured down her face.

He leaned his face close to hers, and his lip curled in disgust as he spoke. "I have tried for years to find true love. When I saw your face, I thought I had, but you were unable to make intelligent conversation. How could you satisfy me? My mind is so far above yours."

"Do you plan to tell that to the citizens outside?" She turned her face away from his. "They will not let you hurt me."

"I will tell you what you must do, *dearest.* You will walk with me out on the balcony and smile and wave to the men like everything is fine between us."

Feeling his breath on her face made her feel waves of nausea. "No, I will not pretend."

He twisted her arm a little more.

"Ouch—please stop!" she said through clenched teeth.

"I will, if you promise to wave to the crowd," he said.

"I promise, just let me go," she said, feeling tears pour down her face.

He loosed his grip on her arm. "Very well, but if you refuse, I will break your arm."

After he moved away from her, she looked at the huge red mark he left and massaged her arm to get the blood flowing again.

"Are you ready, *dearest?* We must calm the crowd now." He held out his arm to her.

"Your Majesty, give her a moment!" Letitia came toward them with a frown.

"Oh, she will be fine," he said, as a sneer twisted his thin lips. "She is a wonderful actress. When we were married, she pretended to love me."

Louise stamped her foot. "I did love you."

"See," he said, pointing a long, thin finger into her face. "I could look in your eyes and imagine you are truthful."

*I shall do what he wants so I can leave.* She lifted her chin. "I am ready now!"

Swallowing hard, she put a hand on his arm, and together they strode to the French doors. Servants saw their intent and opened the doors wide. Together, Louise and Duke Ernest stepped onto the balcony. In the darkness they could not see the faces, yet a hurrah went up. Ernest waved and smiled.

Louise gulped and smiled too. She raised a hand to wave. *Lord, I must not get sick. Ernest will hurt me.*

Suddenly the crowd burst into a hymn.

The men sang every verse. Louise breathed deeply to control the desire to gag and keep a smile on her face instead. Her heart pounded, and her muscles ached with tension.

The Duke raised his hand. "I know how strongly you feel about maintaining family ties. The great reformer would agree!"

The crowd cheered. The duke smiled and waved, and Louise followed his lead. At last the Duke took her arm and guided her back inside.

"They did not disperse. Yet, they seem happy." Exhaustion washed across her body.

"Von Hanstein would be able to handle them. He is no longer here, thanks to you."

She frowned. "But they do not seem violent now."

His face, hard like a mask, frightened her. He had a firm set to his jaw, and his lips twisted into a snarl. "Go to your room. A messenger will notify you when it is safe to leave. I might have to call the military."

She fled to the guest room where the servant had taken her bags. There she found Letitia.

"Poor lamb!" Letitia crooned once she saw Louise's face. "Lie down on the bed, and I will massage your temples and your shoulders."

Louise lay on the bed and fell asleep while her maid massaged. At two in the morning, a knock awoke her.

"Your Majesty!" Letitia whispered. "The messenger came. It is now safe to leave. The carriage awaits us behind the castle."

At two-thirty a.m. Louise and her maid, Letitia, got into a small carriage and left Coburg, never to return.

Three months later, Louise sat in her small home in Ambach. No longer able to afford silk, she wore a white-striped muslin gown. Using sketch book and pencil, she sketched the lush meadow outside her window.

"Madam?" A maid in a starched white uniform knocked and then entered.

"Yes?" Louise looked up from her sketch.

"Count Polzig to see you."

A man walked in wearing a dark tailcoat, beige silk waist coat over a white shirt, black cravat, and white slacks. "Your Majesty, or should I call you Louise?"

She dropped her pencil as her mouth fell open. "But she called you—"

"Count Polzig. That is my title," he said. A huge smile dominated his face.

She stood up and giggled while she gazed into his deep green eyes. "Von Hanstein, how did you get a title?"

His green eyes twinkled. "The Duke of Coburg only has a small German province. Men outside his jurisdiction are not deceived about his character."

She cringed. "After the trial I wondered. The men who gave evidence made Ernest look wonderful, and they told wicked tales about me."

He raised a sandy eyebrow. "Those men work for the Duke. They had to exaggerate to accomplish what he wanted. He wanted to be free of you and keep your father's province."

A lighthearted chuckle escaped her throat. "I wondered if all Coburg hated me. The peasants who escorted me back to the city were gracious. If it had not been for their guns, I would have been at ease."

He pointed a finger at her. "Those peasants knew the Duke. They brought guns to protect themselves. They loved you!"

A faraway look came over her face, and she gave a little giggle. "They were so polite that I sensed they cared. Is it possible Ernest married me to get my father's lands? I know now he never loved me, but the lands I inherited are superb hunting grounds."

Von Hanstein grimaced. "Everyone knows how much the Duke loves hunting."

She closed her eyes and bit her lip. "It hurts to know he used me."

"He is a wealthy man who can surround himself with comforts." The Count spread his hands. "He has the ability to get what he wants—even if it is unjust."

"Unjust!" She rolled her eyes. "I cried for days when I heard he fired you. I know you did nothing."

"I knew the risks, my lady." He stepped closer. "I never touched you, but I must admit guilt."

Her blue eyes widened. "Guilt? For what?"

He bowed his head for a moment. "I fell in love with you."

A blush stole over her thin oval face. "Ah! I did see something in your eyes. But as a married woman, I could not hope."

After taking her tiny hand, he planted a kiss on the back of it. "You could not hope then, but what about now?"

She closed her eyes and shuddered. "Now? Now? I am a divorced woman—accused of adultery."

He dropped to his knees. "I happen to know you are not guilty, dear lady."

"What are you doing?" She frowned and squinted.

He smiled up at her. "I plan to beg for your hand in marriage, dear *honorable* lady."

Her eyebrows flew up. "Are you sure that is what you want?"

The Count nodded. "Yes!"

"Then I will tell you my guilty secret," she said with a demure giggle. "I fell in love with you too."

"And now?"

"Yes!"

He stood up and put his arms around her. "Does that mean yes, you love me? Or does that mean yes, you will marry me?"

She nestled her face into his dark jacket, muffling her answer. "Yes! Yes!"

He kissed the top of her head and then leaned down to kiss her mouth.

After he released her, she looked into his eyes and giggled—a light, silvery sound. *I have not laughed with such abandon in years.*

# CHAPTER 3

## *Contagious!*

"Excuse me, madam! A beggar lady is at the front door. She looks sick. What should I do with her?"

Katie Luther, who was kneeling amongst the cabbages, stood with a sigh. While she brushed the dirt off her hands, the morning sun glinted off her red-brown hair. The mingled smells of vegetables and soil lingered about her clothes. She bit her lip and ran her hand over her very-pregnant abdomen. *It's only September, but I heard rumors of the plague. I do not want to infect the family, nor could I bear to lose another child.* Images came to mind of her daughter, Elizabeth, who died during the heat of August three years ago.

"Fritz, I do not see how I can add one more person to my house."

"But what can I do for her?" He frowned and shrugged. Fritz, one of her household helpers, stood at the edge of the garden behind her three-story stone house which sat in the outskirts of Wittenberg, Germany. He had an expectant look in his dark eyes as he looked down at her.

She pressed her lips together. *God commands us to love those less fortunate. What can I do? Fritz will want specifics.* "Offer her some cheese and bread. Then send her on her way."

"I am sure Dr. Luther would approve," Fritz said. He bowed his six-foot frame and scampered back to the house.

She squatted slowly and returned to her weeding. *I should weed the turnips and the carrots. Then I will deadhead the roses.* Although the weather had begun to cool, she hoped to get a few more blooms to brighten her house. Her home, the Black Cloister, was an old monastery. Dark wood floors gave the house a gloomy atmosphere, but flowers brought in beauty and warmth.

Energetic and enterprising, Katie made a perfect wife for the Reformer, Martin Luther. She had an air of confidence, along with good sense, and she was pretty. Her dark blue eyes sat widely spaced in her attractive heart shaped face, and she had shiny red hair that she wore in a loose hairnet called a snood. She wore a loose-fitting blue dress which fell to her ankles, topped by a blue-gray vest which laced up the front.

Katherine von Bora, Katie, was born to an aristocratic family, but her mother died soon after her birth. Her father decided to remarry and placed her in a convent. She grew up there and learned how to read and write—unusual for a lady in medieval times. Since she could not return home, she took her vows at the age of sixteen.

Although her convent sat across the river from Wittenberg, stories of Martin Luther reached her. He had the audacity to question church policies. In 1517, he challenged the church intellectuals to a debate with his Ninety-Five Theses. Instead of debating him, the clergy and pope condemned him. At last, Luther broke with the church entirely. He preached and wrote that men could be reconciled to God through faith. In addition, he also preached that marriage was superior to celibacy. Many clergy and nuns left their cloisters and married.

Country folk had slipped Luther's writings into the nunnery with various gifts and offerings. Katie, who had a shrewd mind, found his arguments convincing and decided she wanted her freedom. Several of her companions agreed with her. Together they plotted with a tradesman to slip them out of their convent in large vats. Nine nuns, including

Katie, managed to escape the convent to Wittenberg and Luther's protection.

All the other nuns married soon after their arrival—except Katie. The man she preferred could not marry her, because his parents disapproved. Other suitors could not please her. She worked as a housekeeper for a Wittenberg family.

As she continued to weed, Katie grimaced and hoped sending the sick visitor away would please her husband. At times his opinions surprised her. She remembered an interaction with him before they married. She had been shopping in the town square, and she met Doctor Luther on his way home.

He raised his shaggy brown eyebrows. "Katherine von Bora, how do you fare today?"

"Well, thank you," she said with a nod. "And you?"

"Fine! Fine! Ach, dear lady, what shall we do with you?" he said. His floppy black hat bounced back and forth as he shook his head. "Is there *anyone* you would marry?"

"If you asked, I would marry you, Doctor Luther," she said and gazed into his eyes.

The minister threw back his head and laughed.

She did not drop her gaze or even flinch, even though she felt her cheeks grow hot.

Still wearing a jovial smile on his clean-shaven face he said, "Madam, do you want to marry a dead man?"

"Excuse me, doctor, but you are *not* dead." She lifted her chin as she spoke.

He narrowed his eyes, and a frown twisted his mouth. "The emperor condemned me—my enemies could burn me *today.*"

"I understand," she said with a curt nod. "I am, however, still willing to marry you."

Luther cocked an eyebrow. "You need a man who isn't an outlaw."

To her surprise, he proposed to her six months later in the summer of 1530. She could still see the detached look on his face as he explained his change of mind. "Never did I consider marriage—even for an instant. I told my father about you, and I laughed at my own joke. But my father begged me to marry, because he wants grandchildren. So, I decided to marry you. I could please my father, and show the world I believe in marriage."

Now Katie and her husband made their home in his former monastery, which their ruler, Duke John, gave them. They had two children, and in a few weeks, Katie would have a third child.

Katie came back to the present as she heard her husband's voice.

Her husband stood beside the thick wooden door that Fritz had entered a few minutes before. He carried an armful of books and wore a dark robe which went to his knees. "Katie? Katie?"

She lumbered to her feet and waved. "Here, Doctor."

He came toward her. "I found an indigent lady at the door, and I installed her in the room on the second floor by the stairwell."

"But that is the room I prepared for the new student who is coming in tonight," she protested. "Is she sick? Fritz was just here talking about a sick lady. I do not want to infect the entire house."

Her husband shifted the pile of books in his arms and frowned. "We cannot turn her out. Jesus died for her."

Katie cringed. "But what will I do?"

"You will take care of her." His eyebrows flew up, and his eyes bored into hers. "I know how clever and resourceful you are. Just look at you. Not many women would garden in your condition. You will think of something. But I must go. I have a lecture." He turned and bustled off.

Katie opened her mouth, but no words came out. Staring at the back of his dark robes, she watched him retreat into the house. She grimaced and looked down at her large abdomen. *Dear God, what am I to do? I am pregnant and about nine weeks from delivery. Doesn't my husband care about me? When we married he told everyone he was not passionately in love. But I thought he loved me now. Besides we have the children to consider. My precious Elizabeth died. How horrid I felt as we buried her precious body in the dirt. I cannot bear to do that again.*

Already seventeen people lived in their house, and another student would come today. She had four teenaged nieces and nephews from her sister's family, her aunt, who had also escaped the convent, a widowed mother along with her offspring, her own children, and university students who paid rent. In order to provide for the numerous visitors and boarders, she had leased farmland to grow livestock and supplement the garden behind the house. And she brewed beer to sell for extra money. Soon she must go and see to dinner preparations, but her husband commanded her to go and nurse an intruder who might very well have the plague.

*I had best finish this job. Maybe I will send Hilda to see about our ill guest. She is new, but she learns fast.* Hilda, a young orphan girl, had just come to live with the Luther family. Katie had found her quite clever and decided to train her as a housekeeper. However, Hilda also seemed to have a knack for nursing, and Katie had been instructing her in administering herbal preparations.

After hoeing and weeding the entire garden, Katie straightened and rubbed her aching back as she admired her work. She looked up to see her Aunt Lena bringing the children. Her aunt held one child in each hand. Strands of her gray hair escaped her bun and dangled about her wrinkled cheeks.

"Katie, the children have been good, but I need a rest." Her fifty-one year-old aunt had been her mother's sister. A stickler for rules, she expected immediate obedience.

"Thank you! Now get some rest, Auntie. You look tired." She watched her aunt hobble back to the house.

"Mama, I am hungry!" Her son, five-year-old Hans, scurried toward her.

His sister, two-year-old Magdalene, toddled a few steps behind, sucking on her fingers.

"Hans!" She kissed him, rumpled his dark brown hair, and then reached for his sister.

"Hongry Mama! Hongry!" Magdalene said.

"We will go inside and get something to eat." She held her daughter's soft body close to hers. Magdalene's soft blonde hair smelled like the outdoors. *They have been awake since six. I should feed them before dinner and put them down for a nap.*

Hans raced toward the house shouting.

"Hans, come back. Let's wash up our hands at the fountain and then go in and eat." A friend of Luther's had found an ingenious way to pipe the spring into various parts of the city. A fountain in their backyard provided water for washing and cooking. She led both children over to the fountain. Her children splashed water all over themselves and her.

"Oh, that is cold water," Katie said as she felt water hit her face.

"Wawa, wawa!" Magdalene said, while throwing water onto Katie's dress.

"WaTER," Katie corrected.

"Wawaaa!"

"WaTER! Magdalene, say waTER!"

*Crash!* The sound caught Katie by surprise, and she looked up. Hans had collided with one of their boarders. The student, Ulrich, stooped over to pick up his scattered books and papers.

Katie, who felt awkward and heavy, grabbed her daughter and waddled as fast as she could to the doorway. "Hans! You must apologize."

She shifted Magdalene so she could hold his shoulder even though he tried to pull away.

"Ach, you got me wet!" Hans screeched.

"Nevertheless, you must apologize, Hans." She frowned at him. "I have told you to watch where you are going."

Out of the corner of her eye, Katie saw Margaret, the kitchen maid, approach. *I wonder what she needs?*

"Excuse me, Ma'am," Margaret began.

"One moment!" Katie scowled at Hans. "Apologize, now!"

"Forgive me," he mumbled looking at his feet.

"Hans, look him in the eye, and say it again!" Katie snapped.

Hans, eyes still downcast, raised his face to Ulrich and mumbled his apology again.

Ulrich grunted in answer and rushed off, holding his recovered books in a helter-skelter fashion.

Katie let go of Hans with a sigh, set Magdalene on her feet, and turned to the maid. "Yes, Margaret?"

"Excuse me, madam, I know you are busy. But a tradesman is at the door selling kitchen utensils and tableware. I know you want to offer utensils to each person at the table. Do you want me to purchase some?"

*Margaret could do it. She knows what to get. Then I could see to the sick lady. But I would rather see his wares myself.* She straightened her shoulders and reached for a towel in Margaret's hand. "May I dry my hands?"

Margaret nodded and offered the towel.

Katie dried her hands and returned the towel as she said, "I will go to the door. Take the children to the kitchen for bread and sausages. I will meet you there."

A few moments later, she stood outside her front door ready to examine the tradesman's wares. "Let me see your tableware," she said.

"Ah, yes! I have some fine pieces," the peddler said. He turned to a wagon behind him and pointed to a barrel of silverware.

She chose a piece and picked it up. *Sometimes spoons have very thin metal, and silverware must be sturdy to stand up to the students. But unlike some I have seen, these do look substantial.*

"I only sell the finest utensils," the peddler said. He stood with his hands on his hips.

"Yes, these are well made. I shall purchase several of these spoons and a couple of sturdy ladles." She paid him and headed toward the kitchen.

"Excuse me, Ma'am!" Fritz stopped her in the hall. "Which barrel of beer goes to the marketplace today?"

Katie stopped and wrinkled her forehead. *Margaret could give him directions after dinner while I check on the stranger. But I planned to delegate her to Hilda.* "Come with me and I will show you, Fritz." Still holding her new purchases, she escorted him to the cellar, where she pointed out the barrels ready to sell. Feeling fatigued from the trip down the stairs and the added bulk of her large stomach, she lifted her skirts and headed back upstairs to the kitchen and adjoining dining room.

"Margaret, please wash these. We can use them today." She handed the new utensils to the maid. Her servants would serve dinner, the largest meal of the day, at ten, and she checked on preparations. In the next room, she supervised her staff as they set up tables—oblong boards covered by muslin. Afterwards, she turned to her children, who sat at the rustic wood table surrounded by bread and sausages.

"Mama! Wook!" her daughter said. She held a piece of bread in both hands and stuffed a large piece into her mouth.

"I see." she smiled at her daughter's bulging cheeks. "Is it good?"

Magdalene nodded, her eyes glowing with pleasure.

At that moment, her husband walked into the room, and she smiled at his handsome face. He had taken off his black hat and robe. He had a strong face, wavy brown hair, and he wore a loose-fitting, white shirt and baggy, dark pants. After he stopped to drop a kiss on her cheek, he said, "How is our sick visitor?"

"As yet I have had no time to check on her," Katie explained. "But I will send Hilda."

He lowered his eyebrows and gave her a piercing look. "I think you should look in on her yourself," Luther said. "Hilda is not as skilled as you are."

"What if she has the plague? She could be contagious," Katie said. "We have already lost one child."

"Life and death is God's business," Luther said. He pointed to her as he continued. "You must leave that to him!"

Katie swallowed hard as Elizabeth's pale face flashed into her mind for a moment, and she heard the rasping of her dying breath. Pain shot through her abdomen, and she felt sweat run down her back. *Oh God, I cannot live through that again.* She sat down and pushed away all the painful thoughts.

"Papa, look at me." Hans made a silly face and then looked at his father.

"I saw that face." He sat down on a stool by the boy. "Let's play a game. You make a sound, and I shall guess what animal makes that sound."

His eyes aglow, their son nodded. "Oi, oi, oi."

Luther wrinkled his brow and pursed his lips a moment. "That one is hard."

"Listen! I will do it again," Hans said. "Oik, oik, oik."

Magdalene, her big eyes glowing, chimed in to make the sound too, "Oooeee, oooeee."

Her husband slapped wooden table. "That has to be a horse." He glanced up at Katie and gave her a knowing wink.

Hans, believing he had fooled his father, howled with laughter. "No, no, no, Papa. It was a pig."

"Ooee, ooee, is pig," Magdalene said, giggling.

He reached over to tweak his daughter's cheek. "That is good, daughter. Now, Hans, try another." He pounded the table. "I will guess the next one."

Hans bounced up and down on the rustic bench "I'll trick you again," Hans said. He wore a triumphant smile. "Just a minute."

Katie was sitting at the table beside her daughter's small chair. "Say, oink, oink, and wrinkle your nose."

Magdalene wrinkled her nose as directed and made an appropriate sound.

"That was good! Do you want some more cheese?"

Magdalene nodded.

She gave her daughter another helping of cheese and then helped herself to bread, cheese, and cider. Even watching the children play with their father, she still could not extinguish the gnawing ache in her heart. At last, Katie spoke up, "Doctor Luther, the children should nap after they eat. Would you ask Aunt Lena to put them to bed? I would like to check on our visitor."

"You and the children will not join us for dinner?" He winced.

"They got up so early, I worry they will be irritable. A nap will refresh them." She nodded toward their bedroom which was on the next floor.

"Ach! I understand." He said as he ruffled his son's dark hair. "They need to sleep. But when you get older, I want you to dine with us and talk about the Bible. Go on, dear, Auntie will help."

She turned her back on the children's laughter and trudged up the stairs to the room where the unwelcome visitor rested. *I suppose I should get a glimpse. Then I can tell Hilda what she needs to do.*

She found her just as she got to the stairwell. Hilda wore a simple cotton dress with full sleeves. A white scarf covered her brown hair.

"Hilda, come with me. We have a sick visitor, and I will need your help," Katie explained as she walked toward the sickroom.

Katie and Hilda entered the room which Fritz had prepared for the new student. A rectangular, green porcelain furnace stood in the corner opposite the door. The room, although clean, had austere furnishings. A simple bed, covered with a thin blanket, sat under a narrow window. Across from the bed sat a straight wooden chair and a small table.

# Contagious!

The moment Katie approached the bed, she saw a young girl in tattered clothes. Her childish face was ashen, her skin seared with heat, and her breathing labored.

"Ach, she must be thirteen. I had no idea she was so young," Katie said, feeling her heart ache and tears gather behind her eyes. She brushed aside the tangled mass of light brown curls and then picked up a filthy hand and looked at the girl's ragged nails. "She is seriously ill. The crisis will come tonight."

"What should we do?" Hilda's green eyes were wide with fear.

Katie looked around the room as she considered the best way to treat the pretty stranger. "Doctor Luther put her in a convenient room. We have a furnace. I think we should keep her warm—dehydrate her so her lungs will not fill with water. It is too late for any of my herbal preparations. Make preparations for a fire."

"Yes, right away," Hilda said. She moved toward the door. "Is there anything else you might need?"

"Bring me some food and a blanket. I shall stay here the rest of the day and all night. Maybe I can get some sleep in this chair." Katie gestured toward the rustic, wooden chair. "And bring me a bucket of water and rags."

"Must you stay here all night?" Hilda asked. Her eyes went from Katie's face to her protruding stomach.

Katie pressed her lips together and shook her head. "Yes, I must try to pull her through. That is, if God wills it. Go ahead and get what I need."

"Yes, ma'am!" Hilda curtsied and left the room.

Alone with her patient, Katie dropped to her knees, and as she prayed, tears sprang to her eyes. *Oh Father, I should have tended this poor child earlier. I could have delegated any of the tasks I preformed today. My sin could cost this dear child her life. Please help me save her. And Father, protect the child I carry. Your will be done.*

She stood up after praying and straightened the bedclothes while waiting for Hilda. But fear kept creeping into her mind. Over and over she prayed, *Father, please keep my baby safe.*

Hilda made several trips to bring wood, water, blankets, and rags. Katie bathed the girl's face while Hilda built a fire.

"Her skin is very fair, but she has been out in the sun for sometime. Her face and neck are sunburned. And she is malnourished," Katie observed with a rueful sigh. "I wonder how long she has been on the street. Where are her parents?"

"Does she…have the plague?" Hilda hovered between the door and the furnace, staying a good distance from the bed.

"No, this is an infectious fever," Katie said. She glanced up to see Hilda cringe. "Remember that Jesus died for her. Both of us must leave our own health in God's hands."

Hilda curtsied, but moved back to the furnace to prod flames which already burned brightly.

"Fetch Fritz. The two of you can bring me enough fuel for the night and fresh water," Katie directed. "Then there will be no further need for your presence. Margaret knows my plans for dinner. You can help her serve the evening meal. The children will be underfoot, but maybe Aunt Lena will help out. Come for me in the morning."

"Yes, ma'am." Hilda rushed from the room.

While she was gone, Katie bathed the girl and noted that she did not respond at all to the cool water.

*Ach! She is so sick. This will be a long night, Father. Give me strength!* She pulled the upright chair close to the bed and eased her body onto the edge.

Fritz arrived and piled firewood in the corner of the room. Hilda brought Katie stew, a thick slice of bread, and a small jug of cider to sip through the night.

Katie thought about the servants as they served dinner. *I hope they remember everything I taught them.*

Time passed. She changed the position of the girl's body and fluffed pillows while she prayed. In her mind she pictured her husband sitting at dinner without her. The sun sank, and Katie had to light a lantern. Her mind went to the dining room, since she knew it was time for supper. The students usually sat for hours and asked Dr. Luther questions after supper. She had seen several take notes of her husband's words.

As darkness filled the room, Katie kept her vigil by the light of the lantern. She added fuel often to keep the room warm. Every hour or so, she bathed the girl's face and hands with cool water. "Dear child, God loves you. Please get well."

About two in the morning, Katie's patient grew restless. She threw herself about the bed and gnashed her teeth. Suddenly she flung the covers around and began tearing at her clothes. Her face twisted with anguish, and she cried out. Arms and legs, tense and stiff, writhed as if she were in torment.

Katie worried she would have a convulsion and rushed to the bedside. *The crisis has come. Father, please help her to live.* Katie began to croon a lullaby while bathing her face. Finally, sweat broke out on the girl's brow, and her body went limp. The girl's eyes flew open, and she flashed Katie a look of terror.

"It is well. You are very sick, but I shall take care of you," Katie said.

The girl seized Katie's forearm with both hands and squeezed.

Katie winced a little, but she relapsed into song again.

Soon, the girl's hands relaxed and then fell to the bed. Then she nodded and closed her eyes. This time she slept peacefully.

*Yes, I think you will be better in the morning,* Katie thought. She untangled the blankets and covered her patient. Then she sat down in the chair and leaned her head against the hard wood. After pulling a blanket about her, she fell asleep too.

Three or four hours later, the fire burned low, and Katie woke with a jerk. Her face was cool, and her neck ached. Waves of nausea swept over her.

*Ach, I thought the sickness was past. The nurse is not supposed to be sick.* Hoping to settle her stomach, she nibbled at a bit of bread.

She thought she could hear Margaret setting up for breakfast. *Oh, dear, I forgot to consider dinner for today. What provisions do we have available? Did the new student arrive last night? I did not give Fritz any instructions about him. I have allowed this child to get all my attention.*

Standing to stretch, she decided to check on her patient. As she leaned over the bed, the girl opened her eyes.

"Who are you?"

"I am Mrs. Dr. Martin Luther." She reached down to take the girl's hand. "And what is your name?"

"I am Maria," she said. "Why...are you so kind?"

Katie raised her eyebrows. "Because God loves you, Maria. Try to rest. When you feel better I want to know all about you." She meandered around the room, massaging her neck. *At least my stomach feels a bit better.*

Suddenly the door flew open, and her husband burst into the room. "Katie? Are you all right?"

Katie ran to him and threw her arms about his neck. "Doctor Luther!" He enveloped her in his arms, and she felt her body relax. After a long embrace, she related her struggle for Maria's life.

"But are you all right?" He held her at arm's length and surveyed her from head to toe.

"I woke feeling a bit nauseated. But I ate some bread, and I am better." Her hand crept to her abdomen.

He caressed her cheek and gazed into her eyes. "Dearest love, I might not survive if I lost you. I prayed for your health constantly last night."

Katie felt tears rush to her eyes. *He does love me.*

He tilted her chin toward his face and kissed her fiercely. His lips released hers, and he smiled into her eyes. "Now, let me see the girl. What is her name?"

"She is Maria," Katie said.

He took her arm, and together they walked to the bed. "Maria?"

She opened her eyes and shrank into the covers when she saw him over her bed. "Wh-What?"

Katie reached over and touched her cheek. "This is my husband. He would like to pray for you."

Her eyes met Katie's for a moment, seeking reassurance. When she saw Katie's nod of approval, Maria said, "Yes, thank you."

Luther knelt by the bed. "Dear God, thank you for preserving Maria's life. Please help us to minister to her soul."

After the prayer, Maria winced a little and then asked, "May I ask a question?"

Luther rose to his feet and spread his arms. "Aye, child, what do you want?"

"Why did she care for me wh-when she is pregnant? She could get what I have and die."

A deep crease appeared between Luther's dark brows. "God gives life, and you are valuable to him. Katie is precious to me, but I am leaving her in His hands. I hope we can show you the love of God."

Maria gaped first at Luther and then Katie with a question in her eyes, but she said nothing.

"Go back to sleep, dear," Katie said. "We will make sure you are safe."

Luther turned to Katie. "Ach, precious wife, come with me and have some gruel for breakfast," he said. "You are my resident doctor. I knew you were the best one to nurse her last night. But I think Hilda can handle it from here. She put the new student in Charles's room, because he went to visit his mother for a few days.

"Good!" Katie turned her head and rubbed the sore muscles in her neck. "I must go down and concoct something for dinner." She grimaced at the thought.

"Oh, I forgot! Prince John brought several pheasants and some venison by after dinner last night. I told Margaret to prepare it for today."

Katie smiled. *Dear God, you answered my prayer before I even prayed. I should not have worried. We live because you provide all we need.* She and her husband left the room arm in arm.

# CHAPTER 4

# The Journey

Alice sat up in bed and covered her mouth to hold back a scream. She drew in a deep breath and tried to stop shaking. *It was a nightmare.* In her dream she had relived the death of her father. Once during her dream, she had seen her youngest son in the bed, instead of her father. *No! That must not happen. My son will not die.* Alice rubbed her eyes to whisk away the painful tapestry, but she could not.

The third child of Queen Victoria of England, Alice had come to Germany after she married Louis of Hesse, a handsome, dark-haired German prince. She had chocolate-brown hair, cobalt-blue eyes, a creamy, almost-too-fair complexion, a thin face, and a very small figure. Her pretty, yet melancholy face radiated graciousness.

She felt her heart pounding, and she reassured herself by looking about the darkened room. Everything remained unaltered. Her husband's bulky body lay asleep beside her, his face turned away. A pewter clock ticked on the cherry occasional table by the bed. She could see the outlines of the heavy cherry armoire and matching ornate chest opposite her bed. Her fingers caressed the white crocheted bedspread. *I must not wake Louis. He leaves again for military reviews tomorrow.*

She eased out of bed and tiptoed to the overstuffed chair where she had placed her blue velvet robe. Before donning the robe, she held it to her face. A gift from her mother, the new robe still had a faint scent of an English garden. While feeling its softness and inhaling its aroma, she felt embraced by her mother. She draped the robe around her body and tightened the belt until it felt snug around her slender waist. Her feet found the matching slippers under the chair, and she crept from the room. Tiptoeing down the stairs, she avoided the squeaky boards. *The children might wake if they hear me.*

When she reached the patio door, she turned the ornate, brass doorknob and emerged into the crispness of the German night. The stars twinkled over her head, while troubled thoughts flooded her mind.

*Papa! If I could only talk to you now! Now I have no idea whether there is life after death. I have so many questions I wish I could ask you. Oh, Papa, how I miss you!* Her eyes brimmed with tears.

Alice knew the nightmares returned because of her anxiety. She was no stranger to suffering. In her eighteenth year, Alice watched her grandmother die and six months later saw her father die. In her eleven years of marriage, her family had lived through two wars. The Franco-Prussian war had just ended. Many friends had died in the war, and others remained crippled from injuries.

Now, her three-year-old son suffered with hemophilia. A mere scratch on his ear had bled for days. The treatments the doctor suggested made him uncomfortable, and none worked well. A few weeks ago, he had caught a stomach flu that had circulated among the townsfolk. He had suffered a prolonged case, with intestinal bleeding. Fear for his life paralyzed her. She could not bear to lose someone else she loved and face the blackness and finality. Heartache drained all her energy. *If I could turn to God, it would help. But I cannot. Professor Strauss has made me wonder if God exists.*

After Alice married and mingled with the common folk of Germany, she was alarmed by their simplistic thoughts about God. Longing for the deep conversations she had enjoyed at home with her father, Alice had sought out Herr Strauss, a controversial author. She had attended his lectures on philosophy and afterward invited him to her home. Six months later, she had introduced him to her sister, Vicky.

For a few moments her mind returned to the past. One evening after dinner, Vicky and Alice gathered in the luxury of Vicky's sitting room while Strauss explained his theology.

Strauss sat in a brocade wing chair. His dark brown eyes twinkled, and he stroked his gray, pointed beard before he spoke. "Jesus was a good man and taught many truths to his followers, but the stories surrounding his life got exaggerated."

"Give us an example," Vicky said. She moved her chair closer and studied his face.

Strauss gestured in the direction of Vicky's well-stocked library. "I am sure you know the story of the storm on the Sea of Galilee. The disciples were in a boat, and a storm began to batter the ship. They called Jesus for help. Jesus did not stop the storm. Instead, he comforted the sailors. The story was later recorded as a miracle, because Jesus was able to bring such reassurance during that storm."

"What about the feeding of the five thousand?" Vicky said. She glanced at Alice and raised her eyebrows.

"The disciples bought food while Jesus passed out the food already available. Later the writers wanted to demonstrate the wisdom Jesus gave the gathered crowd. Writers created a fable, because Jesus fed their hearts as well as their bodies. Those myths had underlying truths, and we can learn from those truths today. Once we remove the miraculous, we can understand the deep meanings," Strauss answered with a gleam in his eye.

"Your ideas are interesting, and they coincide with other German philosophers today. You have saved us from superstition," Vicky said. Alice remembered Vicky had pursed her lips and raised her chin the way Papa did when he produced a convincing argument.

*Vicky is clever—like Papa. I do not know what I think, but I am afraid Vicky is right.*

A light breeze brushed across Alice's face and brought her mind back to the present. "If Strauss is right, that means our loved ones are… gone." Alice had spoken aloud, but she stopped and turned when she heard a sound behind her.

"Frittie! Why are you awake?" Her stomach lurched. She reached down to pick up her youngest son. His name was William Frederick, but she called him Frittie. Each time she picked him up, anxiety gnawed at her soul. Even the lightest touch on his skin left a nasty bruise.

"Mama," Frittie said, sinking his face into Alice's fluffy robe.

"You must go back to bed," Alice whispered into his soft, brown hair. Caressing his paper-white skin, she worried that loss of sleep would endanger his fragile health.

Frittie touched her face. "Mama, are you crying?" Frittie asked.

"Yes!" Alice said. "Sometimes I think about my Papa, and I miss him," she said. "You will miss your Papa when he goes off to the soldiers, too."

"Will they have war again?" Frittie asked.

"No, the war is over," she said. "Papa won't have to give orders, so he will come home soon."

"Good!" Frittie said.

She was glad that he felt reassured. But turmoil seethed in her heart. Anxiety for her husband, his family, and friends had left her weak. She pictured wounded soldiers who still lay in her hospital. Many lingered in pain somewhere between life and death.

"Let's go back to bed," Alice said and turned toward the door. She carried Frittie up to bed and remained outside his door until she heard his regular breathing. From experience, Alice learned she had to unwind after nightmares, so she repeated her quiet trip downstairs. This time she went to the kitchen. At the stark metal sink, she filled the tea kettle with water. After she lit a fire in the wood stove, she settled herself on a tall stool by the stove to wait.

While the tea kettle heated, she carried on a conversation with herself. "If I could just *discuss* Strauss's ideas I could find mistakes in his reasoning, but I cannot think of anyone who could give me counsel."

She rose to her feet and paced the room. Her hands, which she clasped together at her waist, squeezed so hard that color drained from her fingers. "I tried to get Louis interested in the problem. But so typical of him, he found a spot on his sleeve. 'This needs cleaning,' he said and left the room."

"Mama is no better. She scolded me. She has no opinions and nothing helpful to say. Papa guided her on intellectual questions."

The kettle whistled, and Alice prepared tea and added milk and sugar. She sipped the fresh tea and sighed as she savored its warmth and delicate flavor. As she held the warm cup in her hands, fatigue swept over her body. Sometimes she reviewed the children's lessons when a nightmare kept her wakeful, but two days earlier she had returned from a trip. Once the Franco-Prussian war ended, her husband allowed her to make her long-coveted trip to Italy. The six-week journey, though exhilarating, drained her stamina. *I should go to bed. I should not overtax my strength.*

After she finished her tea, she ran water into the sink to wash the dishes. Alice, influenced by her father, did not cling to her exalted position and hated to leave an extra mess for the cook. Once she cleaned up her tea things, she walked back to bed.

Her husband was snoring when she entered the bedroom. After she silently removed her robe and slippers, she slipped under the covers and snuggled into her pillow with a sigh. *Louis, I wish you could guide me!*

As the sun peeked over the horizon that May morning, Louis rose, leaving his exhausted wife asleep with her anxiety. Dressed in his dark-blue uniform, medals, knee-high boots, and sword, he clomped down the stairs. He made so much noise that he woke both his sons, who slept in the room at the top of the stairs.

In the boys' bedroom, five-year-old Ernest, his brown hair rumpled, sat up in bed. He looked toward his brother's bed which sat opposite his and tilted his head toward the stairs. "I hear Papa!" He threw off the blue-and-white quilted bedspread and slid from his child-sized metal bed onto the patchwork rug on the floor. He scampered into the hallway to the banisters at the top of the stairs. On the floor below his father consulted with a manservant. The rising sun streamed through the windows and sparkled on the enormous sword at his side.

"Goodbye!" Ernest said just as his father disappeared out the front of the house. His small body stiffened to give a parting salute—like his father did. With a sigh of disappointment, he turned on his heel and marched back to his room, where he rummaged in his toy box to find a toy sword.

Frittie, awake but still sleepy, lay nestled in the comfort of his own bed and caressed his pallid cheek with a blanket. He watched his brother dig into the toy box.

"Let's play war!" Ernest said. He brandished a wooden, toy sword.

At the sight of the sword, Frittie's eyes lit up, and he tossed aside his blanket. He jumped out of his bed and dove under it. Once he located his own sword, the two boys engaged in a mock battle.

Victoria, their oldest sister, peered into the room. Her disapproving frown resembled Alice's. Like her mother, she had long, dark hair—at the moment it was disheveled. She wore a long, wrinkled nightdress. "You are much too loud. No one can sleep with that noise. Irene, Ella, and I are awake, but Mama has just returned from her trip. She needs rest."

"Mama will not care," Ernest said. "She wants us to be brave soldiers."

"She does not want you waking her up," Victoria said with her hands on her hips. "Nurse will return soon, and she will be angry." Their nurse did not live with them since Alice had to be budget-conscious.

"Let's go see Mama and say good morning," said Ernest. He dropped his sword and dashed down the hall. His brother followed.

"Ernest, Frittie—" Victoria said. The boys had already rushed into Alice's room.

"Mama!" Ernest called out as he bounced on Alice's bed.

Frittie trailed behind. He climbed up to kiss his mother's face.

"Ernest, Frittie, my dears. Good-morning," Alice said. She suppressed a yawn and smiled. "But, careful Frittie, don't fall, my dear." She tried to sound calm, but when Frittie had almost slipped to the floor, he had frightened her.

"We will play now," said Frittie. He and Ernest slid off the bed and ran chattering around the room. Alice listened as they clamored off, and she smiled at their energy.

Just then the maid appeared with a tea tray. She set the tray on a chest by the window and opened the shades. "Good morning, madam. Would you like the window open?"

"Yes, please open all the windows. A breeze would be pleasant."

The maid nodded, opened the window, and moved to the next room to do the same.

Alice had slept well after returning to bed, but she still felt groggy. Glancing at the pewter clock by her bed, she noted the time. Christa Schenk, her lady-in-waiting, would not arrive for another thirty minutes. Turning on her side, she pulled the covers around her neck and began to drift off to sleep again.

"Frittie, hello! Frittie!" Ernest said.

She gasped when Ernest leaned out of her open bedroom window to yell at his brother. "Ernest! No!" Since her sitting room sat perpendicular to her bedroom, the children could peer out of the bedroom window into her sitting room window. Ernest waved at Frittie, who had just entered her sitting room. She leaped out of bed and pulled Ernest back.

She shook her finger at Ernest. "You could have fallen. You must not be foolish."

Ernest grimaced and looked down at the floor.

With a deep sigh of relief, she climbed back into bed.

However, Frittie followed his brother's example and leaned out the open sitting room window to wave at Ernest. He leaned too far.

"M-Mama! Mama!" Ernest said. "Mama! It is F-Frittie! He fell! He fell!"

In an instant she was at the window. A sharp pain seared through her stomach. Frittie lay silent and still on the flagstone below.

"No!" Alice screamed. "Almighty Father help me! Somebody help me!" She scrambled into her robe and dashed down two flights of steps, tying the belt as she ran. Outside on the patio, she turned to the right and hurried to the place where he lay. "Frittie, Frittie, my dear! You are still alive!" she said while searching his body for injuries. She saw no visible bleeding, but she worried he could be bleeding inside. His face was ashen and his breathing shallow. He did not move even though she called his name and rubbed his hands. Her chest felt tight. *I must think! I am not just a mother, I am a nurse like Florence Nightingale.*

Ernest ran through the house shouting the news, and servants gathered around the victim, hoping to help. Their faces wore serious expressions as they peered at his unconscious figure. Alice glanced up at the growing group of servants and children who gathered around her and spotted Herr Schneider, the butler.

"Herr Schneider, please contact the doctor," she said.

"Right away, Madam!" Herr Schneider bowed and went back into the house.

"Beth, get warm water, a sponge, smelling salts. And I shall require writing materials for keeping records."

"Yes, Your Majesty," Beth said. She curtsied and hurried off.

"Frederick, carry him to bed—carefully!"

She followed behind Frederick as he carried the boy to bed. Her feet felt heavy, and each step took effort. All the color left her already-pale face, and her stomach ached. Once she and Frederick settled Frittie under the covers, Beth arrived with the requested tray of supplies.

"Thank you, Beth," Alice said. "Place the tray on the chest by the bed, where I can reach it easily."

Herr Schneider arrived with a straight chair from the office. "I sent a message to the doctor. And I thought you might need this chair."

"Thank you!" She directed him to move Ernest's bed further toward the wall to allow ample room to work and turned toward her patient. With gentleness, Alice sponged his face with warm water, held smelling salts to his nose, and called his name. Frittie did not respond.

Forty-five minutes later, Dr Eigenbrodt arrived. A tall man with a dark complexion, his pensive chestnut eyes brimmed with concern. A shorter man stood beside him. Both men carried black bags.

"Your Majesty, I brought a colleague, Dr. Schmidt," Dr. Eigenbrodt said.

She offered her hand and gave him weak smile. "Thank you for coming, sir."

"I understand your son had an accident," Dr. Eigenbrodt said.

She bit her lip. "Yes! He fell from a window."

"How far did he fall?"

She cringed. "He fell two stories and landed on pavement."

Dr. Eigenbrodt frowned and pressed his lips together. Both men moved toward the bed. One of them pulled out a reflex hammer and stethoscope.

Alice stepped away from the bed and watched the prolonged examination with worry-filled eyes.

Dr. Schmidt moved further from her and spoke in a low voice. "He does not react to deep pain."

Alice gritted her teeth. *He doesn't want me to hear. I am just a woman, and he thinks I will get hysterical.*

"He is a hemophiliac," said Dr. Eigenbrodt in a husky voice.

"There is no way to stop the bleeding and the pressure." Dr. Schmidt shrugged.

Waves of nausea washed over Alice. *Talk to me! You think he is going to die!*

"Has Dr. Luft found any useful preparations?" Dr. Eigenbrodt asked as the men moved to the door.

"None. We could try Dr. Adler, but—" Dr Schmidt sighed and frowned.

Alice clapped a shaky hand over her mouth. *Please tell me something. Give me some hope!*

"Time is short. Someone should contact the father," Dr. Eigenbrodt said.

"We have sent a messenger," Herr Schneider said. He stood at the door to offer assistance.

*They are worried enough to summon his father. When Louis arrives, they will talk to him. I wish I were a man!*

Alice strained to listen as the men moved out of the room. She walked back to the bed and caressed her son's forehead with a heartbroken sigh. Her muscles were taut with anxiety, she forced herself to think. *I must keep careful watch.* Every fifteen minutes she recorded Frittie's vital signs. With growing alarm, she noted that his breathing became uneven.

*Please, do not leave me, Frittie!* An experienced nurse, she recognized the process of death. *I cannot live through this—again.* As the sun departed over the horizon, her son took a final deep breath, and his body lay still. He was dead. Her slim body crumpled beside the bed into mournful sobs. Louis, who returned shortly after Frittie died, carried his wife from the room as tears streamed down his face into his coarse beard.

The next few days were a blur of tears, funeral plans, telegrams, condolences, and more tears. Alice could sleep only when exhausted. Her slim face was chalky, and her eyes red and swollen from constant weeping. Her ladies-in-waiting encouraged her to rest. But she had to greet the titled guests who came to pay their respects. She did her duty, but at times, she struggled just to stand.

Alice's mother could not attend the funeral. Instead she sent Bertie, Alice's oldest brother, and the Reverend Frederick Robertson.

Several days after the funeral, Alice, accompanied by Christa Schenck, took Reverend Robertson to her hospital. Her mother would have disapproved of Alice's visit. Immediately after a death, Englishmen went into mourning and stayed out of the public for weeks. But she wanted him to visit one patient in particular, Lieutenant Baum, who spoke English. The nurses described his fear and despondency and asked her for advice. Since she battled doubts about God's existence, she had no comfort to give, and she hoped her mother's minister could reach out to his troubled heart.

The smell of antiseptic and starch surrounded them as they entered the hospital ward. Rustling of the nurses' floor-length skirts mingled with an occasional moan from a patient as they moved past iron beds. Alice pointed out changes Florence Nightingale had suggested to the building. Although Alice could not address her patients' spiritual needs, she took great pains to meet their physical needs.

Finally, she brought the minister to the narrow bed where the emaciated soldier lay. Caught in the crossfire during a skirmish, the lieutenant had received multiple injuries. Doctors had to amputate one leg. His battered body refused to heal, and infection threatened his life. Constant suffering had etched deep furrows onto his once-handsome face. Dark circles around his sunken eyes and heavy bandages on his head and arms testified of his agony.

"Lieutenant Baum, I would like you to meet a minister from England." Alice gestured toward the tall, gray-headed clergyman. "His name is Reverend Robertson." She then spoke to the minister. "Lieutenant Baum fought courageously, but he paid dearly for his valor."

"I am sorry to meet you under such sad conditions, but it is always good to meet a brave soldier," Reverend Robertson leaned over the bed and extended his hand.

"I do not feel courageous now," Baum said. He gave the pastor's hand a weak squeeze. "The infection continues to spread." He sighed and closed his eyes. "I may not live. I have horrible nightmares of death and blackness."

Reverend Robertson raised his eyebrows. "Are you prepared to face God?"

Baum hesitated and winced from a fresh wave of pain before he asked, "Tell me sir, and do not lie to me. Is there truly life after death?"

"Yes!" Robertson said. His voice boomed with assurance. "The apostle Peter said, 'We have not followed cunningly devised fables when we made known unto you the power and coming of our Lord Jesus Christ, but we were eyewitnesses of his majesty.'"

Baum sighed and closed his eyes. "I should wish to believe that, sir."

"You can believe it. Peter recorded his testimony in the Bible, the Word of God. Despite the threat of a martyr's death, the apostle did not alter his testimony."

Baum frowned. "Peter suffered a martyr's death? I failed to hear of that."

"Yes! How many men would sacrifice their life for a lie?"

"I daresay none."

Feeling like an intruder, Alice motioned for Christa Schenck. Both moved toward the nurses' desk at the end of the room while the two men talked. After a few moments, Robertson knelt by the bed. She watched the patient's haggard face relax. When the minister concluded his prayer, he and the soldier talked in muted tones. Baum smiled when the minister rose to leave.

On the ride home, the clergyman chatted with Christa Schenck about the fine horses which pulled their carriage. Alice said nothing. As the carriage swayed back and forth, her mind mulled over Robertson's words. *Cunningly devised fables. That is exactly what Strauss calls the stories about Jesus. Peter was a witness who wrote what he saw.*

A week later, the guests were gone, and home life had returned to a predictable routine. Each morning, Alice listened for Frittie's footsteps and with a pang realized he was gone. She missed his warm kisses and gifts of wildflowers. Her thoughts returned often to the family tomb where his body rested. One evening, after her lady-in-waiting retired, Alice sat down in her office to think and find some comfort. She picked up a letter from Strauss which had just arrived. After ripping it open, she read:

Dearest Princess Alice,

I offer my deepest condolences to you and your dear husband. I know the pain must be wretched. However, your son suffers no more. He does not demand your tenderness and care. Enshrine his memory in your heart. Now that he has departed, draw your remaining children into your embrace. Please accept my heartfelt sympathy.

Sincerely,
David F. Strauss

Alice flung the letter across the room. "I do not want Frittie's *memory* enshrined in my heart. I want him back." She burst into tears. Like a sudden thunderstorm, fresh grief raged—as if Frittie had just died. She sobbed until her body was limp.

Eventually her tears subsided, and she blotted her face with her lace-bordered handkerchief. *Is there truly a God—an Almighty God? Is there one who cares and feels our pain? If so, where is he? Why does he not bring comfort to me?*

She thought of Strauss and his arguments. He had not spoken of the comforting God. *If there is no all-powerful God, then there can be no divine compassion for us in our needs. What do I believe about faith in the Almighty?*

"Papa always said Scripture would prove itself. It is logical. Strauss taught that miracles are contrary to nature and therefore illogical. He said Jesus did not perform miracles. Instead, his followers exaggerated stories about him and created myths."

She sighed and rubbed her hands over her face. "The two men contradicted each other. Papa told me a miracle is beyond our understanding, but not irrational. He said an all-powerful God would have control over nature."

Frustration boiled up, and she pounded the desk. "I cannot resolve this! Frittie, I miss you. The searing pain in my heart is too intense. I cannot think! Oh God, I must have help! If you are there, please help me. Do you exist? Are you real? Please help me!"

A memory popped into her mind. "Reverend Robertson mentioned eyewitnesses. I remember reading about witnesses who saw Jesus after the resurrection."

Alice pushed back the chair and walked to the bookcase opposite her desk. Her Bible, buried under several books and coated with dust, sat on the bottom shelf. With eager hands, she brushed away the grime and returned to the desk, where she searched the once-familiar pages. *I found it!*

> "...he rose again the third day according to the Scriptures, and that he was seen of Cephas, then of the twelve. After that he was seen of

above five hundred brethren at once, of whom the greater part remain until this present."

(1 Cor. 15:4–6 KJV)

"This does not sound like myth. The writer speaks of *five hundred* living witnesses. English courts only require one or two witnesses to prove a fact. Evidence forces me to conclude Jesus is alive." Tears slid down her cheeks.

She gasped. *The resurrection!* "How could I have forgotten? Papa spent hours with me before my confirmation. One night his secretary interrupted us because France threatened to invade Italy. Papa told him to come back later—our discussion was more important. After the secretary left, Papa explained the sign of the resurrection. When Jesus started his ministry, the religious leaders asked him for a sign to prove his teachings. Jesus told them he would 'destroy this temple and in three days I will raise it up.' Papa said the resurrection fulfilled the sign."

A frown spread over her brow. "Strauss would say this is a miracle and not logical. But God would be there, and I should have comfort in all life's sorrow. I know what Strauss would say. He would make the words mean something else—a spiritual meaning, leaving me without hope. I want hope!"

Warmth flooded her heart. *Papa and Frittie are not gone forever. They are together in heaven. Almighty Father, forgive me. I should have asked for your guidance earlier.*

She clasped her hands together and took a slow, deep breath as she considered where her two beloved now resided. "Papa died before Frittie's birth. I wonder what Papa said when they met?" She closed her eyes and imagined her son and father meeting for the first time in heaven. The heavenly image, like sunrise, lit up her face with a dazzling smile.

She reached into a drawer and pulled out a stack of sympathy letters from her mother. Deep concern had prompted her to write Alice almost every day after Frittie died. To symbolize mourning, her mother had used paper bordered in black, but the letters contained hope. She had written about Jesus and his resurrection. "Mama, you are correct. I know you could not debate with me, but you tried to guide me back."

Alice stood straighter and taller than she had since her son died. Frittie had loved music, so she had not played the piano since he died. As she walked toward the piano in their drawing room, she searched her memory for the piano composition her father wrote for Psalm 100. Today she wanted to play it again.

"Precious Savior, please tell Papa I came back. It was a tedious journey, but I am safe now. He will want to know." Alice played.

> Make a joyful noise unto the Lord, all ye lands.
> Serve the Lord with gladness,
> Come before his presence with singing.
> Know ye that the Lord, he is God.
> It is he that hath made us and not we ourselves.
> We are his people and the sheep of his pasture.
> Enter into his gates with thanksgiving and into his courts with praise.
> Be thankful unto him, and bless his name.
> For the Lord is good; and his mercy is everlasting,
> And his truth endureth to all generations.
>
> —Psalm 100 (KJV)

# CHAPTER 5

## Whispers

Caroline Bauer closed the paneled oak door of her apartment with a determined click. She sank into a brocade settee as tears coursed down the wrinkled skin of her once-beautiful face. "I have never wearied of acting," she said aloud to her imaginary audience. "I have just completed another matinee—at my age. But I am exhausted by the whispers and the sidelong glances. I am *not* a wicked woman."

At last, she brushed away tears and stumbled to the window over her desk. As she opened the red damask curtains, the afternoon sun streamed into the apartment, bouncing off the mirror over her fireplace, crystal whatnots on the mantel, and the silver frame that held her mother's photo. She nodded, "That is much better. Always bring in the sunlight."

She stopped for a moment and ran her hand over her forehead, disturbing the gray curls around her face. "Maybe there is a way. I am sworn to silence in life, but not in death."

A fresh twinkle lit up her faded blue eyes, and she walked to her French provincial desk. There she located paper, grabbed her pen, and opened her ink bottle. She held her pen aloft and puckered her brows and spoke again to her audience before she wrote, "My story began in 1828."

Caroline did a double pirouette in her full length mirror, bowed, and then launched into the dance she had done the night before. The tiny bedroom had little room for dancing, yet here in front of the mirror, her mind returned to the stage. Her blonde curls bounced with delight as she poured herself into the dance.

Bang!

*Oops! I broke the lamp by the bed.* She knelt down by the occasional table and started to clean up the mess.

"Caroline? What happened?" Mrs. Bauer, her mother, stood at the door with a frown on her face.

Her eyes glazed over. "Mama, I was dancing before the prince again. And I saw him smile at me."

Mrs. Bauer frowned, shook her head, and stooped to pick up the glass. "Be careful, dear. When you start dancing, you forget yourself. You have broken your lamp and spilled oil on the wood floor. We must clean this mess."

With a glow on her face, Caroline dropped onto her bed. Her small, rectangular bedroom was not lush—except for the ornate brass bed, a gift from her late patron, Lady Fuller. "But Mama, it was Prince Leopold from your home—Coburg, Germany. His story is so romantic. Even though his wife died eleven years ago, he still grieves for her. How odd that he would come to *my* performance."

Her mother, who held a fragment of glass, turned to gaze at Caroline. "You are sure? It was really Prince Leopold?"

"I saw him, Mama. He had dark hair and was so handsome." She sat up and put her feet on the hand-crocheted rug by her bed.

"Let me get a broom and the dust bin for this glass. I shall only be a moment." Her mother left the room.

Caroline walked toward the mirror. At twenty-one, Caroline was a German actress and had high cheek bones, creamy white skin, and an oval face set off by luminous blue eyes.

Her mother, from whom Caroline inherited her blonde curls, returned with a small broom, rag, and dustbin.

A playful smile danced across Caroline's face. "Mama, tell me about Leopold again."

Her mother paused and propped the broom against the wall. "He and I played together as children. Even as a child, he was handsome, with all his dark hair and noble face. He fell in love with Charlotte. She was the only child of George IV and heir to the British throne. They were married such a short time. She died in childbirth, after she gave birth to a stillborn son. My nephew, Christian Stockmar, works as Prince Leopold's secretary."

"And Prince Leopold never recovered?" Caroline's eyes had a dreamy look.

Her mother swept up the glass and knelt to wipe up the spilled oil. "I have not had contact with him for years, but that is the rumor. Remember, dear, I was just a playmate—not an aristocrat."

Caroline went to the large wardrobe which sat opposite her bed, opened it, and pulled out the glittery red costume she had worn the night before. Holding it up to her body, she posed in the mirror, and smiled. "I think I cheered him up last night. I saw him smile."

Dustbin in one hand, the broom and rag in the other, Mrs. Bauer said, "You could see him while you danced?"

Still gazing at her reflection in the mirror, Caroline said, "He was in the huge box to my left. It was easy to spot him. He looks just like they described him—dark and melancholy."

"Did you hear that?" Her mother said, tilting her head toward their front door. "Is someone knocking on the door?"

"Yes! I'll get it." She tossed her outfit on the bed. Then she danced out of her room, through the small apartment to the door. She opened it to a man wearing a dark green uniform.

"My name is Huhnlein," the chubby man said. "Prince Leopold wishes to visit actress Caroline Bauer."

"Yes," Caroline said. A sunny smile lit up her face. "I am Caroline Bauer. Please tell the prince to come up." Then she turned to her mother, who had followed her to the door, and whispered, "Mama, it's the prince."

"This is quite an honor." Her mother smiled and fluffed Caroline's blonde curls. Then she slipped an arm around her daughter's slender waist.

"Prince Leopold," the servant announced with a solemn bow.

In a moment, Prince Leopold stood at the door. Holding his tall frame erect, he strode into the tiny room. He had a small mouth, long oval face, prominent nose, and large, chestnut-colored eyes. Towering over the ladies, he wore a knee-length wool coat buttoned up to his chin against the December wind.

Caroline felt a chill go up her spine. She and her mother bowed.

"Caroline Bauer?" he said, examining her with his eyeglass.

"Yes, Your Majesty," Caroline said.

"Your performance last night was superb."

"Thank you, Your Majesty," Caroline replied with her eyes on the floor. "I am honored."

"I believe you are my former playfellow?" He smiled at Mrs. Bauer. "You look well. Stockmar sends you greetings."

"Thank you." She smiled. "I hope Christian is well?"

"Ah, yes! I had hoped to speak with your daughter alone." His dark eyes bored into Caroline, and he dismissed Mrs. Bauer with a wave of his hand.

"Of course, Your Majesty. I shall wait in the next room." Leaving the door ajar, she threw Caroline an anxious glance.

"Your Majesty, please sit here," Caroline pointed to their austere sofa and hoped he did not notice how worn it looked.

He sat and motioned for her to join him. "Come, please, sit here, beside me."

She perched on the opposite end of the couch and glared at her hands, which lay clenched in her lap. Waiting for him to speak, her face burned like fire. At last she looked up to see his sad brown eyes studying her face. "S-Sir? D-Do I displease you?" she asked.

"No! I find you ravishing!" His pensive eyes peered into hers. "Are you in love with anyone?"

"No!" She said trembling. "Many men have admired me over the years."

"Yes?" A deep line furrowed his brow.

"But, I r-refused th-them all," she said. She squeezed her hands until the knuckles turned white.

"Could you love me?" he inched closer to her. His dark wig looked stiff, and she detected creases around his mouth. "You have stirred my heart."

"I don't know," she murmured trying to scoot away. She began twisting the edge of her sleeve. *I did not realize how old he is.*

"I am royal by birth, but I am exhausted. I have searched for a lady to devote herself to me—as my wife. Could you go away with me and live secluded forever?"

She felt his breath on her neck, and she cringed.

"I will keep you safe and love you, sweet lady. If you marry me, I can give enough income to make you comfortable."

*A prince wants to marry me?* Caroline thought of her meager salary. Her brother had just asked for another loan, but costumes were expensive. A pile of bills awaited her even now. She focused on his dark eyes again and saw an expression that made her heart quiver.

"I can—try to love you." Caroline blushed and looked away.

"Ah, you are so lovely." His massive arms crushed her in a long embrace.

Trembling from head to toe, she sat straight and stiff in his arms.

"Fetch your mother," he commanded when he released her.

Caroline jumped up and rushed to the adjoining room.

"Mama!" Words exploded from her mouth. "He asked for you." She began to twirl around and to hum. "He wants to marry me."

Mrs. Bauer frowned. "What?"

Caroline giggled as she did a pirouette. "He wants to talk to you."

"My dear, you must be mistaken—"

"Mama, go talk to him," Caroline said as she performed a curtsey.

Mrs. Bauer, a frown on her pretty face, had to lift her black skirt and step with care to avoid her daughter's toes.

Once her mother had left the room, Caroline tiptoed to the door, which her mother had left open.

"Your Majesty," Mrs. Bauer asked, as she entered. "You wanted to see me?"

The prince had a far-away look in his dark brown eyes. "She is the image of my dead wife."

Mrs. Bauer bowed her head and frowned. "My Caroline looks like Princess Charlotte?"

"Seeing her took me back—" He clenched his jaw and wrinkled his forehead.

"What can I do for you, Your Majesty?" Mrs. Bauer spread her hands.

His long fingers massaged his temples.

"Your Majesty?"

After a long pause, he faced Mrs. Bauer, raised his eyebrows and spoke. "It is possible that your daughter will be the answer. I cannot live alone, but I could not find a companion who would surrender herself to me. I shall have Stockmar write you."

"Your Majesty," Mrs. Bauer said, frowning, "what are you proposing?"

He stood and waved toward the room where Caroline stood listening. "As my wife, she would be my lifetime companion. But she must leave the stage and live concealed from the world."

"Then you speak of a *secret* marriage?" Mrs. Bauer asked. Her brown eyes opened wide.

"Yes," The prince moved toward the door. "Stockmar will give you details."

Mrs. Bauer winced. "I doubt Caroline understood that, but I shall explain."

Before she could say anything further, he swept from the room.

"G-Goodbye, Your Majesty," she said, looking at the already closed door.

"Mama!" Caroline skipped into the room. "I heard him. He wants to marry me!"

"My dear, your beauty touched him deeply, but his plans seem odd. I see no reason why your marriage should be secret." She shook her head. "We must see what Christian advises as head of the family. He has an excellent reputation, and he will not lead us astray."

Two weeks later, they received a letter from Christian Stockmar. He asked them to make arrangements to visit family in Coburg so he could discuss the proposal. Mrs. Bauer followed instructions, but she expressed concern. Caroline, on the other hand, drifted about the house singing love songs all day.

Mother and daughter arrived in Coburg and checked into the obscure inn on the outskirts of town that Stockmar had recommended. Several hours later, the ladies were sitting in their threadbare room when they heard a knock at the door.

"Mama, it's the prince," Caroline said giggling. She assumed a glamorous pose she had been practicing while her mother walked across the rustic floor to open the door.

"Christian, come in." Mrs. Bauer frowned when she saw his thin frame, but she waved her nephew into the tiny room. "We expected the prince."

"You thought the prince would come here?" Christian raised one eyebrow. "No, he will not be seen at a place like this."

"Then why did you ask us to come to this dreadful place?" Mrs. Bauer said wincing. She offered her nephew a straight chair. "Prince Leopold is proposing marriage. Why must it be secret?"

Stockmar eased himself into the chair. "The Prince must be cautious. His mother would forbid this marriage, should she hear of it."

"His mother, the Dowager Duchess?" Mrs. Bauer's eyes grew wide.

"Yes, you must not underestimate the power of his mother. She is a clever lady," Stockmar said. He pursed his lips. "In addition, the Prince could lose his income."

Mrs. Bauer, who stood in front of a bed covered with a moth-eaten quilt, said, "What?"

"He received a salary for life when he married the Princess. However, the English might take exception to another marriage. They could discontinue his salary," Stockmar said with a glance in Caroline's direction.

"Then why does he pursue such a plan?" Mrs. Bauer's face wrinkled in concentration.

"After his wife died, Leopold suffered for years. Now he longs for companionship. I must keep him from the wrong company. Leopold is prepared to endow a large sum on Caroline when they marry, but she must agree to secrecy. However, I must warn you. Leopold is trying to get the Greek throne. If he does, Caroline will not be suitable as a wife." He gave her a searching look.

Mrs. Bauer's face reddened. "King of Greece?"

Stockmar shrugged. "It is unlikely he will succeed."

"When can I see him?" Caroline asked hopping up and down.

"Tomorrow, I will take you to see Prince Leopold," Stockmar said.

"Ah, yes!" Caroline squealed with delight and threw herself onto the rickety bed.

"Hmm." Stockmar gazed at her and pressed his lips together.

"Christian, tell me," Mrs. Bauer said with a shrug. "We need your advice. This secret marriage sounds a bit odd. Should Caroline agree?"

Stockmar focused his piercing blue eyes on her face. "I want the best for you both, and the stage is a risky profession. Leopold will give her income for life, but the marriage must be secret. People could come to the wrong conclusion."

"This makes me uneasy." Mrs. Bauer bit her lip and frowned. "Of course, we need the money, and he treated us kindly."

"Can Mama stay with me when we marry?" Caroline asked hugging herself.

"Oh, yes," Stockmar said. "He expects your mother to come. You must decide if you trust me to look after you."

"Caroline," Mrs. Bauer said wagging a finger in her face, "This is a big decision. I shall advise you to think it over."

Caroline sank onto the couch, wearing a dreamy smile.

Mrs. Bauer sat down beside her and stroked her cheek. "A prince wants to marry my daughter. He sees how lovely you are, and I know you are wonderful."

The next day, Stockmar took Caroline and her mother to a secluded hunting lodge in the woods. Once they had removed their warm clothing, he ushered the two ladies into the sitting room. French armchairs, a loveseat, and a heavy, dark chest sat before a huge, stone fireplace. The room had dark, exposed beams, and mounted deer heads hung on the paneled walls. Leopold stood facing a blazing fire.

"Sir, I brought Caroline and her mother," Stockmar said as he waved the ladies into the room.

The prince turned toward them. He wore a dark frock coat, white shirt, white silk cravat, white pants, and leather boots up to his knees. His dark eyes swept over the ladies. "Mrs. Bauer, it is a pleasure."

She bowed. "Your Majesty."

"My dear Caroline," he said.

Caroline bowed. "Your Majesty."

Leopold took several strides until he stood in front of her. He placed a gentle kiss on each cheek. Then he kissed her lips, gently at first, and then with passion.

Caroline's body trembled as his lips released hers. Her cheeks burned, yet her tongue seemed frozen.

"Dearest, your ravishing face has haunted me since I saw you last." He waved her toward the brocade cushions of the loveseat. "Come and sit beside me."

Her eyes glued to his welcoming smile, she walked to the loveseat and sat down.

"Closer, my dear," the prince said. His dark eyes peered into her soul.

She looked at the narrow strip of cushion which separated them and felt hotter still. After she scooted an inch or so closer, he encircled her with his arm.

He leaned over and kissed her cheek. "Ach, you enchant me. How I shall lavish jewels on you. We shall purchase the finest silks and ermine to transform you into a princess."

Never before had she been at such a loss for words. She looked down at her simple white muslin dress and wished for something nicer. This morning her dress had seemed impressive. Her mother had purchased the figured white muslin at an excellent sale. Then she fashioned it into a gown that matched the latest style—high waist, scoop neck, gathered skirt with frills around the hem, and full sleeves that fastened at the wrist. Even the pretty lace sewn along the edge of her sleeves seemed paltry next to his expensive wool and silk.

"Picture this, my love." He waved his arm. "We sit together in a country home. The sun streams through the window, and the birds sing in delight. A pianist plays a concerto on a huge grand piano. You are resplendent in a gown of brocade, sitting on cushions of velvet. My son plays at your feet, while I read you a sonnet to express my love for you."

She closed her eyes and nodded, her heart trembling with delight.

Two hours later Stockmar, Mrs. Bauer, and Caroline stood at the carriage door, just outside the cottage. The large, ornate carriage had just swept the Prince away.

Mrs. Bauer kept glancing toward the road where Leopold's carriage had just gone. "It seems wrong to keep this marriage a secret. Please advise us. Should Caroline marry the prince?"

"This is a good opportunity," Stockmar said, touching her arm. "She will not be pretty forever. The stage has its dangers too."

"Yes," Mrs. Bauer said. "She loves it, though."

"Will you trust me?" Christian asked, seeing the concern on her face.

"Yes," Mrs. Bauer said, dabbing her eyes with her handkerchief.

Stockmar gazed at Caroline with his piercing eyes. "Will you trust me, Caroline?"

She giggled. "Yes, I shall."

"I will contact you in the spring," Stockmar said, helping the ladies into the carriage. "Hopefully, there will be no obstacles."

When November winds swept through the English countryside, Caroline and Mrs. Bauer resided in Regent's Park, a large park on the outskirts of London. They found their situation much different than expected. In July of 1829, Stockmar arranged a simple ceremony in the cottage where Leopold had deposited the ladies. An Anglican minister came, read the marriage ceremony, and offered a simple prayer. A short honeymoon followed.

Caroline burst into her mother's plush sitting room, where her mother lounged on a French settee with her feet propped on a velvet ottoman. "Mama, read this!"

"What is it?" her mother mumbled, opening the letter. "Oh, dear! The Prince has forbidden you to ride in the park anymore. Someone has seen you."

"What a crime!" Caroline said tossing her blonde curls. "It was my only recreation." Her face was red, and she wore a deep frown. "Ach-h-h-h! Why did I come here?"

"I should consult Christian." She frowned and placed the letter on the mahogany occasional table by her side. "This is extreme."

"Yes, and he has not been here in three weeks," Caroline said.

She posed her body to imitate Stockmar. "Trust me," she said in a low voice, raising one eyebrow as Stockmar often did. "I want the best for both of you."

After she dropped her impersonation, Caroline tramped toward the window, threw open the shutters, and looked out at the imposing shrubs which covered the window. "I can't even see outside! I love sunshine, and the windows should let in the sunshine."

"Now Caroline, let us try to accept—"

Caroline slammed the shutters and a bit of wood came off in her hands. Tossing it aside, she burst into tears.

"Caroline!" Mrs. Bauer rose and embraced her. "Let's talk to the prince," her mother suggested. "We will remind him you need exercise."

"At least the prince came yesterday." she threw herself on a Chippendale chair beside the chintz-covered canopy bed and covered her face with her hands. "I played the piano for him until my hands ached."

At dusk, the prince drove up in his carriage. Enveloped by coats and numerous scarves, he looked like a walking mummy. Caroline peered at him from the sitting room. She pursed her lips with disdain as he eased along the path to the door.

"You're so afraid you'll get sick," she said. "You don't realize you look silly."

"I need to go right to the fire," he demanded upon entering the sitting room. "I detest this biting wind. Come get my things, Caroline."

"Good evening! I hope you are well," Caroline said with exaggerated politeness.

He dumped his wraps into her hands. Once he settled himself on the walnut settee, he peered at Caroline's face with his eyeglass.

"Your cheeks got sunburned," he said. "I knew horseback riding was a mistake."

"What!" She felt her face get hot. "I have to see sunshine. Shut up in this cottage, that is impossible."

"Stay inside," Leopold commanded wagging his finger. "It will ruin your skin."

"Ach-h-h-h!" Caroline trembled with rage.

"Ah! My lady is having a tantrum." His face broke into a smile, and his brown eyes danced. "Calm down, now lass. I want you to continue reading the book you started when I came last."

Caroline bolted from the room and slammed the door behind her.

To Caroline's surprise, servants arrived a week later. They moved her and her mother to a large mansion in the countryside.

She stood in the grand entrance hall, overwhelmed by the inlaid wood floor, beautiful statues, and grand staircase. "Mama, the maid told me this is Claremont House. This is where Leopold lived with Princess Charlotte."

Her mother chuckled. "I sent numerous, frantic letters to Christian. They must have had the proper effect."

"Let's explore!" Caroline said, her eyes gleaming.

Most of the furnishings still wore white dustcovers, but Caroline wandered about the house while the staff opened each room. The sitting room had four sumptuous couches, a marble fireplace, and a grand piano. She strolled about the library, studying the shelves filled with leather-bound volumes. A morning room at the back of the house fulfilled her need for sunshine. It had floor length windows all around and French doors led to a cobblestone patio.

"Mama, come look." Caroline grabbed her mother's black sleeve and pulled her down the hallway. Just outside the library, Caroline stopped in front of a life-size painting in a gilded frame. It was a princess who wore a dress with a crimson bodice and short, puffed sleeves. "The butler told me this is Princess Charlotte. She did resemble me."

"Yes, she did." Mrs. Bauer bit her lip and frowned. "Don't you have a dress like that one?"

"Yes. It is the one I wore when I played the Spanish princess." Caroline's eyes narrowed. "I could dig it out of my trunks."

"Madam," the butler said. "You have a visitor." He ushered the ladies into the sitting room.

"Christian, it is good to see you," Mrs. Bauer said, her brown eyes glowing.

"Good afternoon!" Caroline said with a curt nod, her mind still on the painting.

Stockmar bowed, "Good afternoon, ladies. Caroline, you have color in your cheeks."

"Christian, you look pale." Mrs. Bauer inspected his thin frame, lowering her eyebrows.

"It is my confounded stomach." Stockmar touched his abdomen with a grimace. "Between my indigestion and my lungs, I will not live."

"I'm sorry," Mrs. Bauer said. "I hope you called a doctor. Even though you are a doctor, you can't prescribe for yourself."

"No! These English doctors would kill me." He glared at her with his clear blue eyes. "I can look after myself."

"Dr. Stockmar," Caroline said, impersonating a wealthy woman. She looked down at him, raised her eyebrows, and exaggerated her pronunciation, "Have you considered my health? I *cannot* survive penned up."

"Caroline misses the stage," Mrs. Bauer said, shaking her head. "She feels like a prisoner."

"I engineered your move to Claremont," Stockmar said, raising an eyebrow. "I knew you'd enjoy the change, and I can see improvement."

"Ah, it was your idea, then. The prince would never have considered me. He only cares about himself," Caroline complained. "He pays no attention to me. When he visits, he makes me play the piano or read. Often he brings fabric from which he picks the gold threads for hours. It is an appalling habit."

"Yes, I believe that is called drizzling—a very popular pastime with these wealthy folk. I can speak to the prince about how he treats you," Stockmar said, squinting his blue eyes. "But I shall not be able to end his drizzling."

During the next few weeks, Leopold traveled and did not visit. However, Stockmar entertained them. He came daily, read to them, told jokes, and kept the atmosphere of their home light and cheerful. Mrs. Bauer inquired about the prince and his journey.

"He should be back next week," Stockmar said. "I shall remind him to come by as soon as he returns."

At last, Stockmar sent a note to Caroline alerting her to expect the prince about dusk.

*I wish I could make him notice me.* Caroline mused, crumpling the note. *I know! I could wear the Spanish dress.*

Scurrying into the storage room, she shuffled through trunks until she found it. She draped the dress over her arm and darted to Charlotte's portrait. *My embroidery is a bit different, but the scooped neck, puffed sleeves, and empire waist are all exact.*

Since they had arrived at Claremont House, she had queried the servants about Charlotte. Now she would get details. How did Charlotte move and talk? Caroline would go onstage again tonight—as Leopold's dead wife.

At dusk, a servant came to say the prince had arrived and was waiting for her in the sitting room. She stood before the mirror in her huge dressing room and practiced her facial expressions once more.

Caroline ambled into the sitting room. Leopold stood with his back to her at the marble fireplace, wearing his scarlet uniform.

When he turned and saw Caroline, he froze.

She inclined her head and extended her hand for a kiss. His face turned white. After several moments, he yanked out his eyeglass to inspect her. She felt as if his dark eyes penetrated her inner being.

"Leopold! A kiss?" Caroline raised her brows. She gave him Charlotte's crooked smile and mischievous wink.

"Enough!" he bellowed, raising his chin and looking down at her. "You have prettier hair than Charlotte, but she had a nicer complexion. Your nose is smaller, and your figure is better. But her eyes were much more charming." He flicked his hand as if pushing her away. "However, Princess Louise surpasses you both."

"Who is she?" Caroline's face flushed, and her stomach lurched.

"Her father is the King of France," he said. "I will marry her when I get the throne of Greece."

"What?" Caroline's mouth fell open. "Are you looking for a wife? You are married to me!" Anger twisted her face into a scowl.

"A king needs a royal wife," he said, raising his eyebrows. "You are not royal."

"Greece? Did you say Greece?" She stopped. "I thought you didn't get the throne."

"I am still negotiating," he said, putting his hand on his chest. "But they are preparing to offer me the throne."

"Then I demand a divorce," she said.

"No!" Leopold shook his head and turned his back to her.

"Why not?" She rushed toward him and seized his arm.

"I am not finished with you." He pulled free from her grasp and brushed off his coat.

"You are so cruel," Caroline whispered as tears blurred her vision. Her trembling hands clenched the red silk of her skirt. "Even though I am not a princess, I am a person—with feelings. You treat me like trash." She stomped out of the room and retreated into her bedroom, where she cried for hours.

The next day, Stockmar arrived during breakfast.

"Christian!" Mrs. Bauer rose. "I did not expect you so early." Her face drooped, and she stifled a yawn.

"Good morning! Caroline! Christine!" Stockmar said, giving Caroline an earnest gaze. She had pushed away her plate and sat hunched over her tea cup. Her swollen eyes were focused on the table. "I will pull up a chair. I heard what happened last night." Caroline turned her splotchy face away from his.

"We understood that Leopold lost the throne," Mrs. Bauer said frowning.

"Yes." Stockmar looked down and took a deep breath. "Leopold failed to get the throne, but he continued to negotiate."

"You knew this?" Mrs. Bauer shook her head.

"I did, but I think he will fail." He sighed. "I hoped that his love for Caroline would keep him happy. If she had borne children, his love would be assured." Caroline burst into tears.

"She cried off and on all night," Mrs. Bauer said with a sigh. She ran her hands over her brow. "Neither of us slept."

"I'm sorry," Stockmar reached for her hand. "I'll do what I can."

"When will the divorce be final?" Mrs. Bauer asked, pulling out a wadded handkerchief.

"Leopold has no plans to divorce." Stockmar's face hardened.

"But he said—"

"He does not have a throne, and he wants a wife," Stockmar said with a scowl.

"Will he divorce Caroline?" Mrs. Bauer ran shaky hands over her skirt.

"Yes, if he gets the Greek throne." Stockmar stood.

"What should we do?" Mrs. Bauer asked, reaching for a handkerchief.

"I shall do what I can." He turned toward the door and pointed toward himself. "You must trust me."

"We have done that." Mrs. Bauer got to her feet.

"You should continue. I shall be in touch," he said, raising his voice. He darted from the room.

Mrs. Bauer had raised a hand to ask another question, but she pressed her hand to her mouth.

A shiver ran through Caroline's thin body as she put down her pen. She took a deep breath and addressed her future readers. "Prince Leopold failed to get the throne of Greece. Instead, Belgium offered him a throne, and I finally got my divorce. True to his word, Leopold married the princess from France, and I returned to acting."

She stood and massaged aching muscles in her temples. "People whispered about me. They said I had been a *mistress* to Prince Leopold."

She placed her hand beside her mouth and leaned to one side. "Leopold discarded Caroline Bauer to marry Princess Louise. Did she really think she could keep a prince?"

A grimace on her face, she stood tall and threw out her arms. "I could say *nothing*."

With a dramatic groan she rolled her eyes and paced to the fireplace mantel. "When I entered a room, people would stop talking. They gave me covert glances as if they knew some guilty secret. Just today someone whispered, 'She only services royals.' For years now I have lived with the knowledge of my innocence. The agony is more than I can bear."

Fresh tears coursed down the creases in her cheeks, but she wiped away the tears with the back of her shriveled hand. She strode to the desk. For a moment she caressed her completed story, and then she held the papers to her heart. A smile of triumph tugged at the corners of her mouth as she imagined her story in print after her death. *Yes, my story will be told. People will know the truth—at last.*

# CHAPTER 6

# A Handful of Peppermint Candy

The rhythmic plodding of marching feet—as welcome as an earthquake—broke the stillness soon after sunrise. Already on his knees at that hour, Tom sprang up and rushed to his study window that faced the road. After yanking aside the curtains, he saw the Union army proceeding south toward the mountain. With a grim face, he watched for a few minutes and pondered. He trudged toward the door of his study. Entering the hallway, he hurried toward the kitchen.

Tom—Thomas Hooke McCallie—had a tall, athletic frame, rounded head with light brown hair, a long, slender nose, hazel eyes, well-trimmed beard, and wide mouth. He served as pastor of the First Presbyterian Church of Chattanooga, Tennessee. Chattanooga, his hometown, sat on the Tennessee River, bordered by Lookout Mountain to the north and Missionary Ridge to the south. After the Union soldiers took the city, he had decided to stay, even though most residents had fled. "God called me to Chattanooga, and I will share the gospel with anyone who comes here," he had said to his wife. He lived in a two-story frame house on the outskirts of town along with his wife, thirteen-month-old daughter, his mother, a servant, and two cousins.

The kitchen had a modern wood stove for cooking. Metal utensils hung above a homemade worktable, and a rustic pie safe sat on the far wall.

Ellen McCallie, who stood at the worktable, wore a dark blue muslin gown covered by a white apron with flowers embroidered on the front. She had fastened her pretty chestnut hair in a braided coil at the back of her head. Her charming, oval face had sapphire-blue eyes. At the moment, anxiety showed in her eyes, and she had a deep line between her brows. Just as her husband walked into the room, she dumped flour out of a metal canister into a mixing bowl. "Tom, where do you think the soldiers are going?"

He walked toward her. Once he gathered her petite frame into his arms, he kneaded the knotted muscles in her back. "I think the Union intends to take Missionary Ridge today."

She grimaced and hid her face in his shirt. *Almighty God,* she prayed, *this battle is too close. Please let us leave the city before the battle starts. I am terrified.*

"The battle will be over three miles away," he said. After a few moments, he released her and then tilted her face up to his. "I know you are afraid. I am too. It is uncanny having the battle so close. Remember, God is with us."

Ellen refused to meet his gaze and pulled away. She plopped her spoon into the bowl. A puff of flour rose from the bowl and dusted the table and her arms. "You will have to go into the attic for some flour today. I emptied the canister."

He nodded. "I will do it after breakfast." Tom had put a secret door into their bedroom ceiling which led to an attic store room. In this small storage area, he had hidden their cache of flour and coffee. Then he disguised the opening with a tall wardrobe to protect it from snooping soldiers.

Mrs. McCallie came in holding Mary, Tom and Ellen's thirteen-month-old daughter.

"Da Da!" Mary leaned toward Tom with her slender arms outstretched.

"I think the marching woke her," Mrs. McCallie said.

"Up?" Mary twitched her outstretched fingers.

"Good morning, Mary!" Tom said. He took her in his arms, kissed her, and then transferred her to his shoulders.

Mary, her blue eyes shining, tapped his head. "Go!"

Tom galloped out of the room, snorting and neighing like a horse. Mary laughed.

Mrs. McCallie shook her head at her son's antics. Then she walked out onto the porch, peeking around the corner of the house to observe the marching soldiers. Finally, with a frown, she wandered back to her room.

Ellen, who had stopped working to watch her mother-in-law, shuddered and suppressed a groan. She splashed water over the flour, spilling half of it on the table. With a sigh, she covered her eyes and prayed again, *Lord, I believe you can take care of us. But is my husband right? Is this where we need to be? Mary is so young. I will not complain to my husband, but I am afraid.*

The solemn death-parade continued through their meager breakfast of biscuits and coffee. But once the marching ended, Ellen found the silence disconcerting. She finished clearing up the breakfast dishes and found her husband in his study. "Tom, are they about to attack?"

"I will walk outside and see," he said. "But I want you to stay here. Do not prepare the soup for the soldiers until I return." The McCallie family prepared broth each day and delivered it to wounded soldiers in the hospital.

Ellen's eyes opened wide in fear. "Will you be safe?" Since the Union army had taken Chattanooga, the family stayed indoors most of the time.

His eyes twinkled, and he caressed her cheek. "I will stay out of the range of the cannons."

"But you could be hit by a stray bullet. Aren't you afraid?"

"Yes, I am frightened, but I refuse to give way. I believe God wants me here to give the gospel. I am safer here than anywhere else." He set his jaw and left the room. Hearing him open and shut the front door, she clasped her hands together and squeezed until her hands hurt.

Ellen finished her morning chores and climbed the stairs to her bedroom. *I wonder if I could see Tom? Is he safe?* After raising the shade, she looked toward the ridge. The army had leveled all the trees in the area, so she had a clear view of the mountain. She could see the fiery explosions as the Union soldiers discharged their weapons while charging up Missionary Ridge. Her heart began to pound, and her hand flew to her mouth. But a fascination gripped her, and she could not move away. The gruesome undertaking, called war, happened right before her eyes.

*This is not the first time we have been in danger,* she thought. When the war descended on Chattanooga four months ago, her nightmare had begun.

She and Tom had been visiting her mother in Cleveland, about thirty miles east of Chattanooga. Mary, nine-months-old then, contracted a fever so severe the doctor worried she would die.

Ellen, who had just gotten Mary to sleep, had settled herself on her mother's couch. She picked up her embroidery and put several French knots in the center of a flower. Suddenly Tom, returning from the post office, hurried into the room. His face was flushed.

"Ellen, I have to go back to Chattanooga!" he had said. His handsome face had a stony look of resolve.

"Why, what happened?" Her eyes met his and saw a blaze of determination.

He held up a letter from the man who filled his pulpit while he was gone. "This letter came today. It is from Rev. Palmer. He says that the

Federals have surrounded the city. Last Sunday the Union cannons fired on the city. I need to go back."

Ellen nodded toward Mary's bedroom. "You have to go now? Mary is not out of danger."

He put his hand on her shoulder. "You must remain here with her until she is better. But I must return."

"But you could be killed!" Ellen said, frowning.

He shrugged. "That is possible, but I force such thoughts from my mind. At this moment the people need their pastor. I will pack and leave right away." He turned on his heel and left the room.

The room faded. Her needlework dropped from her hands as her heart fluttered. *He is going toward the conflict. Is he testing God? You should not hold a loaded gun to your head and ask for protection while pulling the trigger. My husband is a good man, but he could be wrong.*

Ellen's stomach knotted up as she heard her husband in the next room preparing to leave. She tried to thread a needle, but she could not hold the thread still. Desperate to fill her mind with something, she grabbed a book that sat on the end table. Her eyes would not focus on the words. She dropped to her knees by the couch. "Almighty Father," she whispered, "I cannot let him go unless you give me strength. Tom is determined. Help me." A tear fell from her eye as she rose. She paced the room, blotting her face with her handkerchief as if pushing back tears.

Later her husband returned to the room holding his trunk. "I am ready to go. I will write when I arrive."

She nodded but did not meet his eyes.

"Ellen?" His voice had an edge of tension. He put down his bag and held out his arms to her.

She ran to him and embraced him. "P-Please, be careful."

At last he kissed her. After a long embrace, he stepped back. Then he picked up his bag and moved toward the door. "I wish you could come. I shall miss you. Goodbye, dearest! God is with you."

The door closed behind him, and she shuddered. *I refuse to give way to tears.* At once she seized four braided rugs which lay scattered about the sitting room. After taking them to the back porch, she found a broom and began to pound them. With each whack her heart cried out, *No! No!* Dust clouds from the rugs brought on a coughing fit and made her eyes water. After finishing the rugs, she went back to the sitting room holding the broom. She entered the room and swept the floor, shoving furniture out of the way as she worked. Exhaustion came at last, and she threw herself into an overstuffed chair. Now she was too tired to worry.

Two days later, she decided to check the mail. She waited until Mary's afternoon nap, so her mother would not have to entertain her. The afternoon sun beat down on her as she trudged to the post office. The hot and sweltering heat of July made the short walk seem longer than usual. She had to pass the church graveyard on the way, and it reminded her of her husband's peril. *I hope Tom is safe. What would I do without him?*

As she entered the post office, she looked around the simple room. The familiar sights gave little comfort. The light green walls needed a coat of paint, and the same rustic bench sat alongside the wall. She walked to the window, her heart pounding.

"Hello, Mrs. McCallie!" The clerk, Mr. Findley, had been there for thirty years. "I have some mail for your mother, but nothing for you."

Ellen swallowed hard and blinked back tears. Her stomach felt queasy. All the way home fears crowded her mind. *Is Tom safe?*

The next day she repeated her journey. This time she quoted Bible verses to keep her mind busy. *I will never leave you nor forsake you. That means God is with me.* Standing in line at the window, she fidgeted with her bonnet and straightened the lace on her sleeves over and over.

A smile lit up the clerk's face when he saw her. "Mrs. McCallie, you have a letter today."

She snatched the letter. "Th-Th-Thank you, sir!" Once she saw Tom's handwriting, she gave a squeal of delight and held the letter to her heart. With trembling fingers, she tore it open.

> Dearest Ellen,
>
> I arrived without incident. The Union army pulled back from the city shortly after I arrived. People are still very anxious, but more Confederate troops poured into the city. City officials have chosen civilian "officers" to stay alert for enemy activity.
>
> I miss you terribly, and I think of you constantly. My prayer is that Mary will recover soon and you can come home.
>
> Your loving husband,
> Tom

Finally, in August, Mary had recovered enough to travel, so Ellen bought train tickets to Chattanooga.

At the train station, the hiss of steam from the train merged with the voices of Confederate passengers. On board she found herself surrounded by a fortress of gray uniforms. One serviceman asked to carry her suitcase. Enlisted men lifted their hats and said, "Hello ma'am!" Several officers smiled at the baby and another offered her a seat.

As the train pulled into the station, she saw her husband. His face glowed, and his eyes scanned the windows of the train, looking for her. Once she stepped onto the platform, he caught her eye by waving and smiling. After many warm embraces, they headed home in the carriage. Driving home, she felt herself smile for the first time in weeks. Confederates stood guard all over the city. Tom had suffered no calamity, the baby had thrown off the fever, and she was home again.

But her feeling of security was short-lived. The day after she returned to Chattanooga, the Confederate army left. She and Tom stood at the sitting room window and saw them march away. Some traveled on horseback, some in crowded wagons, others walked. Although it was August, she shivered as if the warmth oozed out of her body.

Every muscle in her body stiffened when the Union army marched in.

"But Ellen, they walked in without firing a shot. No one got injured," Tom had said.

She looked away thinking, *Should I praise God for the Union army? They are all thieves.* Their blue uniforms had swarmed her yard. They stole everything outside the house, including the contents of their small garden. She saw one man walk away with a chicken under each arm. She watched them pull up her picket fence. Another gang of men carried off their sweet corn. Enlisted men, taking orders from officers, ran off with their grain. Before the day ended, military tents lined every inch of their property. Within a few days, Union soldiers had chopped down their orchard to build breastworks.

A few days later, Tom had come in from a trip to the well. He found his wife at the potbellied stove, and he handed her the bucket of water. "Ellen, the generals are planning some sort of attack."

She picked up a scoop. Dipping water out of the bucket, she poured it into the pot on the stove. "How do you know?"

"They are moving men and equipment toward the south," he said with a grimace. "I saw horses pulling several cannons earlier this week. The men seem a bit restless, too."

*Oh, Father! I do not want to be near a huge battle! Should I ask Tom to take us away?*

"I will have our Sunday service as usual. Pray with me for men to come and hear the gospel." He stroked his mustache.

She turned and looked at his face. His jaw was set. Her lips could not form the words, but her heart cried out, *I want to leave.* She stirred the soup with such vigor that she splashed liquid on her apron.

The following Sunday, the church was full, but not with her fellow citizens. Blue-coated men filled the beautiful hand-hewn pews. She walked down the aisle past them, keeping her eyes on the floor. Once she settled herself on the front row in front of the lush mahogany altar, she clasped her Bible so hard that her knuckles looked white.

The morning sun shone through the arched windows, dancing off the brass candlesticks on the altar. When her husband stood to speak, sunlight glistened on his sweaty brow. He pulled out his handkerchief, blotted his forehead, and opened his Bible. Resolve shone in his eyes as he began, "A war rages in our land. Everyone has divided up between the Union and the Confederates. In the heart of each citizen is the image of the soldier, either in blue or gray. But I ask you today to consider a more serious issue. Where would you be if you died today?"

Ellen kept her eyes riveted on her husband. *You don't have to work so hard. These are the invaders.* Right away she felt a stab of guilt in her heart. She knew that her husband had not been in favor of slavery or of succession. But these soldiers had stolen their food. *Lord, I do not like them. Help them to hear the message today. Then let us leave here and give the gospel somewhere else.*

A few days later, Ellen and Tom saw wagon after wagon of wounded men pass in front of their house. Men with bloodstained bandages, ragged war-weary soldiers with blood-spattered clothes made Ellen feel sick. Some lay in the wagons, others sat propped against each other; their pain could be seen in their waxen complexions and ghastly frowns. The flies, clustering around their bandages, mixed with the dust from the road.

"Ellen, I am going out to get some news," Tom had said while walking toward the door.

She had picked up Mary and turned her face away from the windows. *It must have been a massacre. Protect my dear daughter.*

Two hours later, while sweeping the kitchen, she heard her husband come in the front door. She put aside the broom and went in search of him. "Tom? Tom?"

She found him in his office. He had collapsed into his chair and held his head in his hands. His face was ashen. She rushed toward him and threw her arms around his shoulders "Tom, are you alright? What happened?"

"The two armies fought at Chickamauga, Georgia, which is about thirteen miles from here. It appears the Union lost—badly. The medics emptied our church and filled it with wounded men. I saw a pile of arms and legs beside the front door." He covered his eyes.

"Terrible! This war is just appalling. Why does God allow war?" She stomped her foot.

He shook his head and ran his hands over his beard. His voice sounded exhausted. "Men are sinners. They devise ways to kill each other."

"At least the battle is over," Ellen said.

"The Confederates still hold the mountains. They could drive the Union out," Tom replied.

"You mean there will be another battle?"

"Yes, we will see more action," Tom said. His shoulders sagged.

Ellen closed her eyes and sighed. *I cannot live through a battle. Maybe we will evacuate, since we cannot use the church.*

But neither army took action for two months. Tom and Ellen had some canned vegetables, dried meat, water, and coffee in the attic, but everything else had been stolen. They had little money, but even if they had, food was hard to find. *Lord, will we starve? Why are we here?*

Finally, in November, the Union took Lookout Mountain. Tom had gone out to observe the battle. Ellen tried to ignore the whole episode, but it was hard when the cannons fired. Their explosions shook the house and rattled the windows. Gritting her teeth, she kept busy cleaning, cooking, and playing with her daughter. Besides, her mother-in-law occupied the only room with a window where she could look out and see the battle. Ellen did not feel comfortable intruding on her privacy.

Ellen returned to the present. The shooting ended and the thick, black smoke cleared. *I saw smoky explosions go up the mountain. I guess that means the Union overran the Confederates.* She frowned, wondering if the Confederate forces would attack the city in an effort to retake the lost ground. *What will I carry off if I have to run away? How will we know which direction to go?* Mary's innocent baby face appeared in her mind. She pictured herself running with the baby in her arms while soldiers approached behind her—their guns drawn—and she felt sweat break out on her face. A rustling sound behind her made her jump. She turned to find her husband standing right behind her.

"Did you watch?" he asked quietly. His face was pale.

She covered her face with her hands. "Yes!"

"The Union holds the ridge now." He pointed toward the window.

She swallowed and nodded. A deep frown creased her brow.

With a sigh he put his hand on her shoulder. "That battle is not the important one."

She shuddered. "I do not want to see another battle. I am terrified."

"I know you are dear, but there's more than one battle being fought here. I am speaking of spiritual warfare. The real enemy is Satan, who wants to silence the truth. I stayed here to give the gospel to dying men."

She pointed toward the kitchen. "But the canned vegetables are almost gone. Soldiers stole the rest of our food—except the flour and coffee you hid. What are we going to eat when everything is gone?" Her eyes were wide with fear.

He put his arms around her and placed his cheek on the top of her head. "I guess this is one of those times that we have to live by faith. Let's pray. Almighty Father, we are dependent on you. Fear will make us run from our duty. But hunger will take our lives. Provide courage…and… sustenance." His voice faltered. "Without you, we…cannot live."

*And could you allow us to leave?* Ellen silently prayed. *I want safety. Please God?*

Tom's arms tightened around her. "And…help me to share the truth even in the midst of this dreadful time. In the name of Jesus, Amen."

Three weeks passed. Except for the sparse supplies hidden in the attic, they had nothing to eat but coffee and biscuits. The McCallies had almost no United States currency, but Tom tried to buy food with the money he did have. Several times he went out looking for something to buy, but each time he came home with nothing.

The day before Christmas came. Ellen served hard tack which a kind soldier had brought to their door. The hardships of the past six months flashed in her mind. She compared them to joyous Christmases of her childhood. The jubilation of Christmas seemed so far away. After dinner, she put Mary to bed and cleared up the dishes. Her heart, so full of the hardship, felt weary and sorrowful. She looked down at her hands in the soapy water and cried out to God. *I cannot seem to praise you for the gift of your Son. God will you please help me?* When she completed her chores, she first walked to her bedroom for a sock and then found hammer and nails in the tool box. From there she marched to the sitting room.

Her husband stepped into the room wearing a frown. "What are you doing?"

"I am putting up a stocking," Ellen said. "War or not, this is Christmas Eve."

Tom raised his eyebrows and said, "Go on to bed, my love. I think I will study a bit before I retire."

"Good night then, dear." She nodded and left the room.

Tom listened. His wife proceeded down the hall and up the steps. Satisfied that she had turned to the right at the top of the steps and entered the bedroom, he waited ten minutes longer. Then he tiptoed into the kitchen, picked up a small lantern, and lit it. He donned his heavy coat, which hung on a peg next to the door, and slipped out into the cold evening.

The moment he stepped outside onto the porch, cold wind whipped his face, and flakes of snow swirled around him. He shivered. While he stood on the edge of the porch and gazed into the cloudy sky, he whispered a prayer. "Father, I know you care about our smallest concerns. Help me to find a special gift for Ellen's stocking." He lifted the lantern high and stepped into his yard. Proceeding with care to avoid soldiers' tents, he made his way to the road. The darkened city loomed before him. Several small campfires, surrounded by tents, sat on the edge of the city. A few remaining homes in the city had lights in the windows. Going down the main road, he headed toward the Tennessee River. Since supplies and merchants would arrive on the river, his best chance of finding what he wanted would be there. After he walked several miles, a figure came out of the darkness and stood in front of him.

"It is a cold night to be walking," the man said.

Tom could not see his face, but he could discern the outline of his clothes. He was surely an officer. "Yes sir, it is. But since it is Christmas Eve, I am looking for a gift for my wife."

"You are not a soldier, are you?" the officer folded his arms.

"I am Reverend McCallie."

"Oh, yes! You are the minister we called before the execution last week."

"Yes, I am." Tom grimaced at the memory of the condemned young man.

"Did the man…make his peace with God?"

"I wish I could answer yes. I gave him every chance, but I do not think so," Tom replied.

"You did what you could. Now tell me, what are you hoping to find?" The officer's voice had softened.

"My wife, Ellen, insisted on hanging a stocking. I hoped to find a merchant who would sell me a small gift to drop inside."

The soldier nodded and motioned for Tom to follow. "I can help you there. A merchant came into town this afternoon. He had to come to me for permission to sell to the soldiers. I will take you to him."

The two men walked in silence for several blocks. Then they came upon a small cabin where light streamed from the window. Lamplight fell across the officer's stripes. Tom had been talking to a major. The officer knocked on the cabin door. In a moment, a chubby man with a round face opened the door. He winced when he saw the officer.

"I have a customer for you," the officer said, gesturing toward Tom.

"Yes, sir. Please come in." He waved them indoors. "As you can see, I came from Florida with a fine selection of fruit and several kinds of candy."

As soon as Tom stepped inside the cabin, he smelled oranges. Once his eyes adjusted to the light, he could see that crates of fruit filled the small room. "How much are the oranges?"

"Two for fifty cents," the man said.

The major shook his graying head. "That seems expensive."

The merchant flinched and cleared his throat. "I will give you three for fifty cents and throw in a handful of peppermint candies too."

Tom smiled and reached into his pocket. "It is a deal." He handed the merchant the money. After receiving the fruit and candy, he put them into his coat pockets.

Once he completed the transaction, the two men stepped outside. Tom turned to the major. "I want to thank you for your kindness. My wife will be thrilled about the fruit, and I never expected to get candy."

The major shook his head. "No, sir, I need to thank you. You stayed here and risked your life to minister to these men. I consider it a pleasure to do something for you. Merry Christmas!"

"I plan to have services in my home...once stability returns. I would be pleased if you would come," Tom said.

"I should enjoy attending church again. Thank you!"

The men parted with a handshake, and Tom went home. Chuckling with joy, he entered the sitting room and unloaded his pockets into the stocking. The sight of the bulging stocking brought a prayer of thankfulness. "Thank you. You prepared the way for me. You answered even before I prayed." He returned his coat and the lantern to the kitchen and then climbed the stairs to his bedroom.

Once in the bedroom, he could hear his wife's regular breathing. He stooped over to kiss her cheek and discovered it was wet. He touched the pillow. It was wet too. *The war has kept her very tense. This Christmas must seem very sad, but she will have a surprise.* A mischievous smile danced across his face as he thought about her reaction. He put on his nightshirt and climbed into bed with care so he would not wake Ellen. Soon he fell asleep.

A shrill cry woke him the next morning. He sat up in bed and saw Ellen was gone. Throwing on his robe, he ran to the sitting room, where he found his wife gazing in wonder at the stocking. She pulled it off the mantel and poured its contents on the end table. "Husband! Where did you find these? Oranges! And peppermint candy is my favorite."

He put his arms around her. "The Lord always provides, Ellen. Merry Christmas!"

Tears flowed down her face. "God is so good. My fear kept me from believing he could take care of us. Now I know he can. I know we are right where he wants us."

# CHAPTER 7

## A Figure of War

I *wish I could catch a glimpse of Fritz. He is still so weak. Is he fatigued from the ride? He is still recovering, but he looks so dignified and handsome.* Seated beneath the arched stonework inside Westminster Abbey, Vicky gazed at the throng of loyal British subjects that sat in the audience before her. Her tall, dark-headed husband had made an impressive appearance this morning—in spite of his weight loss. She pictured him in his uniform, covered with metals, plumed helmet, white gloves which flared at the wrist, and his gilded sword hanging from his belt.

Vicky, the daughter of England's Queen Victoria, stood almost five feet tall and had large, charcoal-gray eyes set in a pretty round face. Her maid had styled her dark brown hair in a fashionable coiffure, and she had donned a red silk dress with a scoop neck bordered with gold braid. Surrounded by her siblings, her children, her nieces, and her nephews, she sat erect and regal on the dais just in front of the engraved woodwork of the choir stall. Her mother, dressed in her royal finery, sat in front and center. Fritz, her husband, sat with other family members on her mother's right.

Today the nation celebrated her mother's golden jubilee—Queen Victoria had reigned fifty years. Huge flower arrangements sitting on pedestals at the edge of the platform tinged the air with their sweet fragrance. Large candelabra scattered about the cathedral, blended their light with the rainbow of colors that filtered through stained glass windows. Both cast a flickering glow on the elaborate stonework of the sanctuary and on the crowd. The ladies wore ankle-length gowns, flowered hats, and long gloves. The men wore fine jackets and silk cravats.

*Even if I strained my neck, I am not sure I could see him. People would notice if I leaned over so I could see.* Inhaling slowly, she relaxed and followed the service, which would be safe and predictable. She had lived in constant upheaval the past few months. Not only did she long to see her husband recover, but also she yearned for rest.

Her husband's illness had almost made her sick as well. Doctors had removed nodules growing on Fritz's vocal chords several times, but each time they returned. Several German doctors had dared to suggest he might have cancer of the throat—a death sentence. The press announced the diagnosis as fact and watched their sales soar. Each day they advanced further news about his declining health and added to Vicky's distress. Her father-in-law, Emperor Wilhelm I, was old and could not live much longer. Soon Fritz would ascend to his father's throne in Germany. Vicky could not imagine illness preventing his long-awaited reign. Relying on philosophy and willpower, she had sustained herself while encouraging her weakened and depressed husband.

Hope came when an Englishman, Dr. Mackenzie, had disagreed with the German doctors. His biopsies came back cancer free. Vicky and Fritz came to England a month early for the Jubilee so they could take advantage of Dr. Mackenzie's treatments. After a few weeks under the Englishman's care, he was stronger and able to attend the festivities. Dressed in a white military uniform, he had ridden a white horse in the procession to the church.

Vicky felt love and pride well up inside her as she heard the strains of her late father's *Te Deum* fill the enormous cathedral. *Dearest Papa,*

*I miss you. My childhood was so happy. Papa and Mama loved each other, and their love flowed throughout our home.*

Cherished memories filled her mind. Her father had spent hours preparing her for confirmation and for her political life in Germany. She pictured her wedding when Papa had given her away to Fritz. When she arrived at the New Palace as a bride, Fritz, robust and strong, lifted her off her feet and danced with her in his arms. She could almost feel the pressure of his strong embrace and the roughness of his cheek on hers. Then another image came. She saw again the joy on her husband's face when he learned she carried their first child. This picture was replaced by another—even more exquisite. Fritz sat beside her with their youngsters, Willy and Charlotte, playing at their feet. Her eyes met his—aglow with love and laughter.

The *Te Deum* ended, and her mind returned to the Abbey. Prayers, music, and Scripture reading succeeded each other as the service proceeded. Vicky, weary from wrangling with German doctors, relished the Englishness and familiarity of the service. At last the service ended, and each child and grandchild gave the Queen a bow and a kiss while stepping down from the dais. Vicky, every ounce a princess, played her part well and hid all her concerns. Onlookers would never guess the heartache and struggle she had suffered in recent months.

After the procession returned to Buckingham Palace, Vicky was walking toward the dining area for the family dinner when she saw the prime minister approach.

"Hello, Lord Salisbury! How are you?" Vicky said, smiling.

"Princess Victoria! Excuse me. I should use your married name, Princess Frederick. It is a pleasure to see you here." The prime minister's voice expressed his kindness. "We all wondered if your husband would be able to attend."

"I am glad to say that an English doctor has restored my husband's health, Lord Salisbury," she said with a twinkle in her eyes.

"Then that is an answer to prayer," Lord Salisbury remarked.

"Yes, if you *believe* that God takes the time to listen." Vicky's eyebrows rose.

"Oh, but surely He does, Your Majesty," Lord Salisbury said, nodding. "No one questions that."

"I question it," Vicky blurted out. Lord Salisbury winced, but she continued, "Dr. Mackenzie is a man of science. His work helped my husband."

"Ah! Very good!" He coughed and cleared his throat. "I trust that you enjoyed the jubilee service?"

"Yes, it was English." Vicky's eyes danced. "That is reason enough."

"I hope you enjoy your visit." Lord Salisbury scanned the hallway as if he searched for someone.

"It is indeed good to be home," Vicky replied with sigh and a fond glance about the hall.

"Excuse me, Your Majesty," Lord Salisbury said, stepping away, "I must attend to several matters."

"Of course, perhaps we can talk later." She had caught sight of one of her brothers and longed to catch up on his family.

The June festivities ended, but Vicky and her husband settled at Windsor Castle to take advantage of Dr. Mackenzie's medications and therapy. Three months passed, and she watched with joy as her husband's strength and color improved.

"Fritz?" Vicky, her face creased with concern, had rushed to her husband's bedside with a letter in hand. Her mother had assigned them a plush bedroom in the castle, and Fritz napped on a canopy bed with heavy, green velvet draperies. She pushed back the gray silk bedspread and sat beside her husband. "Fritz? Are you awake?"

"Yes!" His voice sounded hoarse, but his thin lips curled into a smile.

She returned his smile as she leaned over to kiss him. "It is so good to hear you speak, my love. When we arrived you were unable to utter a sound."

He winked at her and then eyed the letter in her hand. "I do not think that is why you woke me. What does that letter say?"

Vicky grimaced. "This is another letter demanding you come home at once."

"How is father?" Fritz raised himself on his elbow and reached for the letter.

"Your father's condition continues to worsen," Vicky said with a shrug as he took the letter. "At the moment you are not needed, but the prime minister and cabinet members become more and more adamant."

"Hmm!" Fritz frowned and ran a hand over his full beard as he read.

Vicky, concern in her eyes, watched him read for a moment.

"I am the heir, and they want me to be there—just in case," he said.

Vicky got up and paced along the Oriental carpet as she gazed at the gilded carvings on the domed ceiling. "We have finally found someone who can cure you, but they insist on taking you from him. Do they want you to die? Or is it because you are going to an English doctor—not a German?"

"I do not think the politicians hate Englishmen," Fritz said, raising his bushy eyebrows. He put the letter aside. "They want *me.* This letter is the strongest appeal yet. In fact, they almost threaten us."

"That is why I brought the letter at once." She bit her lip.

Fritz sat up and offered her the letter. "Perhaps we should start making plans to leave."

"No!" Vicky said, rushing toward him. She snatched the letter from his hand. "You are too close to recovery now, you must not return just as the cool weather comes in."

"What then?" Fritz said with a shrug. "I cannot stay away forever."

She leaned over and caressed his thin, pale cheek. "We return once you are completely well. You have had too many relapses. This time we must be more cautious."

He tapped the paper she held in her left hand. "And what shall we do about these demands?"

"Tell them we are on our way," Vicky said. She walked to a Walnut secretary and pulled a letter from a drawer. "I found a lovely cottage in San Remo, Italy, where we can rest several more months. Warm weather there will aid your recovery, and we will not be in *England*."

"Vicky, dear, I do not dislike England," Fritz said as he eased himself back onto the bed.

"They do!" Vicky said. "They distrust me because I am not German, and they despise English doctors."

He closed his eyes. "No one dislikes you, dear wife. My subjects may be jealous of the doctors here, but they think well of you."

"Do you feel ready to return?" she asked.

"No…I do not," he said with a grimace. After a pause, he said, "Make plans to go to Italy. Both of us can rest a bit more before we go home."

A triumphant smile blazed across Vicky's face as she turned to the secretary and pulled out supplies to write a letter.

One sunny morning in October, the couple took a long walk in the garden outside their Italian villa. The air held the fragrance of flowers, and the birds warbled and trilled. As they strolled hand-in-hand along rows of flowers, Vicky admired her husband's improved appearance.

"Fritz, look at those roses," Vicky noted, pointing out a rosebud still damp with the morning dew. "This reminds me of our first walk in the gardens at the New Palace. Do you remember?"

"How could I forget?" Fritz said. He wore a sheepish grin. "You had me so bewitched I did not care about the flowers."

Vicky squeezed his hand and smiled. She had not felt this happy in weeks.

"But today I think I will sit down and let you describe the glories of the garden." He moved toward a wrought iron chair nearby. Easing his body into the chair, he rubbed his throat and frowned.

"Close your eyes and absorb the sun's warm rays. They will complete the cure," Vicky said. "I will pick some roses and bring them to you."

Fritz smiled but rested his head on his hand.

"Look Fritz, these roses smell wonderful." Vicky returned and pressed several opening buds into his hands. "They remind me of your health—almost perfect."

Fritz cleared his throat and frowned.

"Is something wrong?" she said when she saw him swallow several times.

"Nothing," he said with a smile. "I believe a bit of dust is caught in my throat."

"Ah! You see, we were wise to come here." She patted his hand. "You are not yet ready to face the harsh German winters."

He nodded and grimaced.

A month later, the sounds of a quarrel awakened Vicky in the night. Worried about Fritz, she sat up and pushed back the light blanket. Her husband had been sleeping in a nearby room since his illness, so she lit a candle beside her bed and tiptoed into the adjoining bedroom. His bed was empty. With the candle in her hand, she followed the sounds of irate voices to the sitting room, where she found him in a heated argument with their eldest son, Wilhelm.

Fritz, brown eyes widened in anger, sat on the edge of the sofa, clutching the arm. A small chandelier overhead sent shimmering gas light over the room, but it did not dispel all the shadows on his thin face. Wilhelm stood before the tiled fireplace, where coals glowed and sizzled. With his square jaw set, dark eyebrows knotted in defiance, and arms crossed, he glared at his father.

"You have no right asking my father to give you authority!" Fritz shouted. His lean face was flushed, and he pointed toward his son.

"You are unable to do your job," Wilhelm said, "I can! Someone needs to run Germany. I will do it!" He tapped his chest.

"No!" Fritz stood.

"Wilhelm," Vicky came in from the doorway and stepped between them. "How did you find out where we were? Who let you in?"

"This does not concern you. I am talking to Father." He frowned at her.

"I *am* your mother," Vicky said. "Go away and let your father rest!"

Fritz looked at his wife, and his eyes pled for understanding. "Dearest, he came to me. You must not involve yourself in this."

"Fritz, you show signs of catching a chill," she said with a gentler tone. "You do not need a setback."

"Mother, leave!" Wilhelm yanked her aside, and the burning candle in her hand clattered onto the wooden floor.

"Wilhelm!" his mother screeched as she snuffed the flame and placed the candle holder on a nearby chest.

"Willy, do not treat your mother like that," Fritz commanded. His eyebrows lowered, his eyes blazed, veins protruded in his face and neck.

"This is a waste of my time," Wilhelm said. He turned toward the door. "Grandfather will sign the document giving me the authority—"

"In his condition father would sign anything," Fritz interrupted him. He shook his fist in the air. Suddenly, he swayed and began to cough.

Terrified, Vicky watched as Fritz collapsed onto the damask cushions of the sofa. In a panic, she dashed toward him and patted his back.

"Well, this proves the press is right," Wilhelm announced with a sneer. "Papa is not able to rule. He is dying!" He screamed into his mother's face. "Did you hear that? He is dying of cancer."

Ignoring her son, Vicky hovered over her husband, feeling her heart hammer in her chest. Fritz sat slumped over, coughing and wheezing. His hand covered his mouth, but blood oozed between his fingers.

Vicky rang the bell for the maid. Wilhelm flung open the door and marched out of the room just as a frightened maid appeared.

"Get some cold compresses," Vicky commanded the maid.

"Wake up Dr. Bergmann," she ordered her lady-in-waiting, who arrived as the maid left. Dr. Bergman, a German doctor, had agreed to stay with Fritz while he recovered.

Bleary-eyed and yawning, Dr. Bergmann arrived within ten minutes. He insisted that Fritz return to the bedroom. After he preformed a careful exam, he turned to Vicky with a sigh. "Your Majesty, I stopped the bleeding, so the immediate problem is under control. But I see a new growth, and it looks serious. We must wire Dr. Mackenzie right away."

A few days later, Dr. Mackenzie arrived from England. He examined Fritz. His thin face wore a frown as he put away his tools. "I don't like the look of this lesion." Gesturing to his own throat he explained, "The other lesions I treated appeared to originate from overuse of the voice. What I see now resembles cancer."

"What do you recommend?" Vicky asked, feeling her heart skip. Dreading the answer, she held her body rigid.

"I suggest we take another piece of the lesion and send it to the pathologist for analysis," Dr. Mackenzie said. "But prepare yourself for the worst. Your choices will not be good. Most doctors recommend removing the larynx when tests confirm cancer. Fritz will have to make that decision."

With trembling hands, Vicky massaged her aching temples. She contemplated reliving the surgery and then the endless wait for the report. Since she knew she would sink into depression, she rallied her courage by reciting her favorite philosophers. Later, alone in her suite, she lectured herself and paced to whip up her energy. *Fritz needs me. He will give up if I don't stand beside him and fight. I must get him through this.*

Five months passed. The microscopic test preformed by Dr. Mackenzie never confirmed cancer, but Fritz grew worse. German doctors insisted on removing the trachea to save his life. But Fritz refused. The tumor grew until it interfered with his breathing and doctors had to place a tube in his throat. Newspapers accused Vicky of sentencing her husband to death because she did not trust German doctors.

A few weeks earlier, Fritz had lost his father and was now Emperor Frederick III. However, he was very sick and needed to escape the pressures of Berlin, so Vicky accompanied Fritz to the family's palace in Potsdam.

Vicky chose a bedroom-refuge at the far end of the hall from her husband's bedroom. Heavy velvet draperies on the canopy bed and at the windows muffled the sounds of her bitter sobs. She escaped there when she could no longer hold back. Prolonged sobbing gave her temporary relief.

Sitting in an upholstered arm chair, Vicky whispered her concerns. "Dearest Fritz, I love you. I fear you…will die." Sobs shook Vicky's entire body.

Greta Baum and Hilda Schneider, Vicky's ladies-in-waiting, stood near, trying to offer comfort. Greta had a handkerchief to replace the one Vicky used. Hilda held a glass of water.

"My love, please, please…do not leave me." Her voice broke as she spoke through the sobs. "I do not want to be…alone. I don't want… to be a widow!"

"The Emperor could not have a more loyal wife," Greta said. She patted Vicky's shoulder.

A discreet tap on the door made her jump.

"Please answer, Hilda. We will hope it is not bad news," Vicky whispered. She rose and turned her back to the door. "I don't want to be seen like this."

Hilda opened the door to a wide-eyed maid who curtsied. "Excuse me, I have news for the Empress."

"You may give it to me," Hilda replied.

"Crown Prince Wilhelm has arrived and is in the library."

"Wait a moment," said Hilda. "I will inform the Empress." She closed the door and reported the news to Vicky.

"Why does he have to come here?" Vicky said, squeezing her handkerchief until her fingers were white. "I don't want to see him gloat. Yes, he will be emperor soon."

"Shall I say you are not available?" Greta whispered.

"No, I do not want him to torment the emperor. Tell him I will see him."

Greta moved to the door.

Vicky turned to Hilda. "Who knows what Wilhelm has done now. He is probably still obsessed with the letters Mother and I have exchanged over the years. Somehow he believes she wrote to inform me how Fritz should run Germany."

She paused to think. "Help me fix my face so that I appear…calm."

After Greta spoke to the maid, both ladies accompanied Vicky to her room, where she washed her face over and over with cold water.

Thirty minutes later, Vicky pranced into the library, pretending a cool detachment. But her self-control failed when she saw Wilhelm and several of his men ransacking the desk.

"Wilhelm, what are you doing?" Vicky asked in outrage. As she spoke, he dumped the contents of a drawer on the floor and tossed papers all over the room.

"I am looking for letters," Wilhelm answered, grimacing in her direction.

"What are you talking about?" She squeezed her hands into fists. *You will find nothing. All my letters are locked in Buckingham Palace.*

"I want the letters from Grandmama," Wilhelm said. "I know she gave you advice. Give them to me."

"Mother did not counsel me," Vicky said, shaking her head. "Unless you care about the clothes she thought I should wear."

"How can I believe you?" Wilhelm said. "You have practically killed my father by insisting on British doctors." He took several papers and threw them into the fireplace.

"No! What was that?" Breathing hard, she ran to the fire and tried to snatch the discarded papers, but the fire consumed them. "Stop it now! You have no right to do this."

"I will stop *when* you give me the papers." Wilhelm halted a moment, his smoldering eyes burning into hers.

"Wilhelm, I have nothing to give." Vicky spread her arms wide and shrugged.

"Then I will find them myself," Wilhelm charged to the bookcase and ripped a book off the shelf. He shook it, threw it to the floor, and reached for another book. Vicky dashed to his side and latched onto his arm, but he pushed her aside and continued. Realizing she could not stop him alone, Vicky turned and fled from the room.

Count Seckendorff, the house chamberlain, met her in the hall. Rather than his usual impassive expression, his face wore a pinched look. "Your Majesty, please excuse me. The Emperor asked for the newspaper. The Berlin paper has two articles about the family. One of them accuses you of forcing your will on the Emperor and choosing English doctors. The other declares that the Emperor is already dead and that you escaped here to Potsdam to keep it secret."

Vicky sighed.

Seckendorff cleared his throat and continued, "In light of these articles, I handed the Emperor the local paper, since the material there is more sympathetic."

She covered her eyes a moment with a trembling hand. "You are quite right. Yes, he may insist on the Berlin paper, but keep it from him for now. I am weary of the slander those nasty men print. Evil, evil men!"

"Very good, Your Majesty," he said.

"Oh, Seckendorff," she said, shaking her head. "Please throw Wilhelm out of the library. He should not go through his father's possessions without permission."

"Right away, Your Majesty!" Seckendorf marched off to obey.

Vicky turned toward the sitting room. As she entered, she saw Wilhelm's wife, Dona, sitting by the fireplace. She was taller than Vicky and had light brown hair, a small mouth, and a rectangular face.

"Dona?" Vicky greeted her with surprise. "No one told me that you came."

"Wilhelm said we did not need to be announced. We are family," she said, tossing her mother-in-law a withering expression. "He left me here while he went to find the papers."

*So Wilhelm had burst in without waiting for the staff again.* "Dona, I have no papers," she said.

"Wilhelm was right. He said you would deny everything." Dona's dark eyes squinted suspicion. "If you give them up, it will be easier."

"I do not have anything to give," she replied with a sigh.

"Your mother, Queen Victoria, wants to run Germany as well as England," Dona said, curling her lip. "Wilhelm will not let her."

"This is nonsense." Vicky sat down on a silk wing chair opposite Dona and looked directly into her round face. "Mother has no such idea."

"Soon Wilhelm will be emperor," Dona said, raising her eyebrows. "He doesn't believe in the new ideas about freedom and rights." She gazed at her mother-in-law with a sneer. "He will wield power over the people—for the good of all. He can make life difficult for you." She adjusted her skirt with a smug expression on her face.

"I know about Wilhelm's politics." Vicky said. She closed her eyes and shook her head in disgust.

"Wilhelm told me about you," Dona said. She wrinkled her small nose as she spoke. "You are English. When your husband dies, you will call English clergymen."

"I know several German churchmen who understand modern thought," Vicky replied, raising an eyebrow.

"You confess to believing modern thought? Wilhelm said you don't believe in the resurrection." Dona scowled and shook her head. "He won't allow people to think those things."

Vicky covered her eyes with her hand for a moment. "Wilhelm does not understand," she said. "David Frederick Strauss was a German who had some scientific theories about the resurrection. He proposed several explanations for the resurrection. One theory is that Jesus fainted on the cross and then revived after he had rested in the tomb."

"That cannot be right," Dona protested. "How do you explain the Bible?"

"The Bible must be read with the proper understanding," Vicky said. She raised her chin preparing to explain. "It does contain some eternal truths—like the idea of resurrection. But the reality is in your heart. That is where I hold those who are dear to me."

"What does *that* mean?" Dona said with a frown.

Vicky took a gulp of air and brushed aside tears that came to her dark eyes. "I lost my beloved father after I married. Then two of my boys died. Sigi and Waldy were...good boys. All three of them are with me still—inside."

Dona gave Vicky a scandalous look. "They are inside of you? I do not understand."

A faraway look came into Vicky's eyes as she remembered. "My father was such a dear man, and I treasured every word he said. Sigi loved me so much. He had brain fever and convulsions tormented him until he died. Waldy had a severe fever which destroyed his vital energy. Inside my heart, they will stay with me forever."

"Dona, let's go." Wilhelm burst into the room. "Seckendorff insisted we leave, but I will return. When Papa dies this house will be mine. I will find the evidence that they are hiding." He gave his mother a threatening glare and led his wife from the room.

"Goodbye, Wilhelm," Vicky whispered. *These pitiful people who need to rely on God. He could not be good and kind. Otherwise, He would not have let my father die when I was so young. I was just twenty-one, and he was my mentor. How I loved him. No one could be so cruel.* Her lips trembled as tears slid down her face. She tried to reach for a handkerchief but could not control the trembling of her hands.

Greta and Hilda appeared at the door. After seeing her face, they looked at each other and frowned. "Your Majesty, can we do anything to help?" Greta asked, stepping forward.

"Greta, see that the maids straighten the library." Vicky crossed her arms and hugged herself. "Losing my husband is enough to bear. Then my own son comes and mutilates the library. I cannot bear to see the destruction he left behind."

"Yes, ma'am," Greta replied and left the room.

"Hilda, I would like you to contact an English clergyman named William Boyd Carpenter. Look in my papers and find his address. Send a wire and invite him to come here."

With a nod and curtsy, Hilda departed.

Vicky let out a tiny sob and rubbed her hands over her eyes. *I hope he is able to visit. I need to talk to a modern clergyman who understands science. But now, I must find rest.*

She turned and strolled to the section of the house used only by the family and stopped at a heavy old oak door. With a furtive look up and down the hall, she extracted a key from her skirt pocket and unlocked the door. The hinges creaked and groaned as she pushed open the door. It was a nursery. But a fine layer of dust coated the entire room.

The wall opposite the door had a large window from which sunshine filtered through dust and cobwebs. Colorful blocks, carved wooden animals, and toy train cars lay strewn about the room—as if a child had just meandered away from playtime. A small table with child-size chairs stood on the right side of the room. Several books lay on top of the table. One had been left open, revealing faded pictures of animals. Nearby was a bookcase filled with picture books. The left wall had an ornate iron crib and a Bentwood rocker.

Vicky walked to the crib and pulled away a soft, freshly-laundered wool blanket to uncover a wax figure. When Sigi died, Vicky had used her artistic skill and her mother's eye for detail to make a life-size replica of Sigi. Despite the dust in the rest of the room, she kept the wax doll and his blanket pristine.

"Dear Sigi, how was your day?" Vicky said. "You love Mama. Wilhelm does not. He is mean to Mama." Picking up the wax figure with tender care, Vicky settled herself in the rocking chair. "Would you like Mama to sing? I love you, Sigi. You will never leave me."

She crooned a lullaby as she rocked. Her tense muscles relaxed as peace swept over her soul.

# CHAPTER 8

# Starting Over

The rising sun trickled through slats of the shutters, and Katie Luther, widow of the reformer, opened her eyes. She stretched out her hand to her husband's side of the bed and felt nothing. Pain stabbed her stomach as a strange emptiness echoed in her soul. *Of course, what did I expect? He has been dead almost a year and a half.* Shadows still cloaked the simple furnishings, but her eyes wandered about the bedroom they had shared—as if he might appear. He would pour water from the blue and white pitcher into the matching basin and wash his face. Both sat on the rustic chest across from her bed. In the semidarkness the pitcher and basin looked almost black. The white crocheted runner which hung over the sides of the chest had a grayish cast—like her heart. Her husband would sit on the straight chair alongside the chest to slip on his shoes. She could almost see him there now. Today its thin cushion looked worn and even sad. To her right sat the huge armoire where they stored their clothes. How many times she had seen him there, rustling amongst clothing. Now, it held only her belongings. A tear rolled down her cheek.

Her husband had died in February of 1546. As if the whole world felt his absence, the Schmalkaldic War erupted soon afterward. Charles

V, Holy Roman Emperor, wished to subdue the Protestants once and for all. Seven months after her husband's death, Charles V convinced German Duke Maurice to fight with him against the Lutheran rulers which comprised the Schmalkaldic League. In October, the fighting threatened Wittenberg, and she fled with her children. The Schmalkaldic War raged between Catholics and Protestants for nine months. When she heard the fighting had ended, she packed her bags to come home. Late last night, after dark, she had returned to the Black Cloister, the former monastery that the duke had given to Luther on his marriage.

The July morning was comfortably warm. She pushed away the thin sheet and sat up, putting her feet on the dark wooden floor. The wood felt smooth and comforting beneath her feet. After living here so many years, her feet knew each crack and crevice. She was home again—almost. The empty spot beside her made her heart ache. But then, Dr. Luther would never live here again.

With a sigh, she smoothed her wrinkled nightdress and trudged to fling open the shutters. The rising sun danced through the window as she walked to the rustic mirror that hung over the chest. Her auburn hair, now streaked with gray, hung in two braids. Her heart-shaped face had grown a little chubby, and tiny lines surrounded her deep blue eyes and thin lips. She reached for the blue pitcher and splashed water into the basin. As she washed her face and neck, she wished she could wash away the gnawing pain in her heart. But then, she must keep her focus. Now that she was home, she must rebuild her boarding house so she could support herself and the children. From the top drawer she pulled a rough, white towel and blotted her face.

Gazing into the mirror once again, she saw her lip twist in agony, and she knew a storm would come. She buried her face deep in the folds of her towel as sobs cascaded from her soul. Her whole body cried. Even her toes seemed to heave with her sorrow. At last, the tears spent themselves, and she put the towel beside the basin.

She completed her morning toilet and went back to the bed, kneeling on Luther's side. With folded hands and bowed head, she poured out her soul, "Oh Almighty God, I need your strength. I must rebuild. This house must give us a living like it did when Doctor Luther lived. Please help me! I can hardly think now that I have returned. Yet there is much to be done. My children need food and clothes, and I must earn it. Boarders paid the bills before, and they must again. The gardens will provide food and provisions to sell. But I will have barriers. Deliver me from the guardians who will hold me back. I need your help!"

As she finished her prayer, a scratching sound at the door caught her attention, and she rose and opened the door. A gray and white dog bounced in, wagging his tail. "Herr Faustus! I did not see you last night and thought you must have died in the war."

The dog yelped in delight and licked her hands.

She reached down to scratch his ears. "You remember the good times don't you? The house was not filled with dust, but filled with people."

The dog's warm brown eyes gazed into hers as he danced at her feet.

"Come Faustus!" she said as she settled herself in the straight chair.

He followed her in delight and sat at her feet, cradling his face on her knees.

"Doctor Luther was such a good man, and while he lived theologians and godly students filled our home. My farms provided meat, vegetables, and even food to sell. I could take in the poor to share God's love. We had an abundance of love and money. But I had to keep the good doctor from giving away everything we had." Her thin lips curled into a smile. "Remember the silver platter? He intended to give that to a friend, but I wanted to *use* it. I devised storage places so he could not impoverish us with his generosity."

The dog tilted his head as if agreeing with each word.

Her blue eyes got a faraway look. "He loved me so much, and we slept in this room—in that bed—for almost twenty-one years! Right over there I gave birth to six children. Two of them are in heaven with their father."

The dog whined and made her feel he understood.

A tear rolled down her cheek, and she brushed it aside. "When my husband felt affectionate, he called *me* Doctor Luther. Now, he knew I had no training, though I read widely and tried to learn from real doctors. He told me I could handle his health better than any doctor on earth."

Faustus thumped his tail on the floor with delight.

"With God's help, I did manage to cure him a few times. Our student boarders sat around the table each night after supper asking questions about the Lord. I saw many taking notes, and I hear that several call those discussions 'table talk' and want to publish his words."

The dog's warm tongue flicked over her toes, and then he lay at her feet with his nose on his paws. He kept his brown eyes fastened on her face.

"Aye, but he would scold me for grieving so!" She sniffled. "The memories are just so precious."

The dog raised his head and thumped his tail.

"But I must not sit here," she said as she rose. "Come with me. There is work to be done. I suppose I must begin by writing letters to ask for funds. I detest the job, but I must have money. I shall start with the King of Denmark. He has sent us money in the past."

Faustus followed at her heels as she bustled out of the room.

Dressed in a dark skirt and vest laced tightly over a loose blouse, Katie scurried into the marketplace with a basket in her hand for provisions. Familiar scenes and the chatter of old friends brought a sigh of contentment. The stately gothic church where her husband had preached begged to have its stained glass windows washed, but it had suffered no harm from the war. Her husband's statue, wearing clerical robes and standing with his arms around the open Bible, stood in the square just as it had before. The blacksmith had died in the war, and his shop stood dark and empty. But the old oak where her husband had burned the papal decree against him stood untouched, raising its huge branches to sunshine. She had just seen a local farmer and placed an order for wheat when she saw her brother-in-law, Jacob Luther. "Hello, Jacob! How are you this fine morning?"

"Ach! Katie!" Her brother-in-law closed the distance between them. "Seeing you delights me. What business brings you to the market?"

Katie looked up into his clean-shaven face. "I must order provisions. I was fortunate enough to meet Herr Schnell to place an order for wheat."

Jacob ran a hand through his wavy gray hair. "Provisions? Do not buy too much, dear sister. You will not have a boarding house to run."

Katie felt her heart skip when she caught a glimpse of Jacob's hand. His short, stubby fingers resembled her dear husband's.

"Katie?" Jacob's long, thin nose twitched, and his dark eyes held a look of concern when she winced.

"Sorry! I just felt a bit tired." Katie looked down and smoothed the fabric of her skirt while she gathered her composure. "But I did order enough for boarders. I must earn a living."

His square forehead wrinkled. "But dear sister, you did not consult me. And you know I am one of your guardians."

She gritted her teeth. *Yes, I know! Doctor Luther did not want me to have guardians.* "Jacob, you know how much freedom your brother gave me. I can be trusted."

He wrapped a lanky arm about her shoulders. "He did a wonderful job caring for you. But now I have responsibility for you. You must consult with me."

She nodded. "I did plan to consult, but I did not want to lose the opportunity. Schnell's grain is particularly fine."

"I do hope you plan to make and sell your beer." He winked at her. "No one else can make it as well anywhere in Germany."

A smile spread across her face. "Thank you! In fact, I do intend to sell beer again. And I plan on restocking the farms with animals."

His jolly expression collapsed into a frown. "Oh, but that would far exceed your income! I fear you must be cautious."

*I can earn enough to cover my expenses.* She bit her lip to hold back a retort. "I will discuss this with you anon. Right now, I must finish shopping and get a meal prepared for the children."

"Kiss all of them for me, Katie! Get busy and feed those young ones!" He turned and walked away.

*And that is just one of my guardians! How shall I get anything done?*

"Katie! Katie Luther!"

She turned to see Doctor Ratzenberger, her cousin on her father's side and another of her guardians, coming toward her. He had helped her husband with his research and served as medical advisor to the former duke. Now he wore a broad smile on his heart-shaped face, and the wind tousled his gray and auburn hair.

"Matthew! What a pleasure!"

Her cousin grabbed her and gave her a crushing embrace. Then he held her at arm's length and looked up and down her figure. "Someone told me you had returned last week. I am most pleased you arrived safely."

"Actually we arrived last night after dark and collapsed into our beds." She gestured toward the Black Cloister. "Today I need to buy enough to feed everyone."

He raised his craggy eyebrows. "I hope you plan on bringing in boarders again?"

"Yes, I do!" Katie smiled. "And I want to sell beer again."

"You do make fine beer, Katie." He put one hand on her shoulder. "I would love to drink some again, but in the absence of your husband, I think you take on too much. As your guardian, I think Luther beer should be a thing of the past. In fact, you probably ought to find a smaller house that would cost less to maintain."

Katie sighed and threw up her hands. "A smaller house would not work. I need room for students to board."

A deep frown creased his brow, and he stepped back, putting his hands into his pockets. "My concern is for you, Katie. You know how much I respected your husband. And you are family. A woman can get in over her head when it comes to business."

Katie leaned toward him and wagged a finger in his face. "Matthew! You know my husband trusted me. He studied, and I did the business. All he ever did was sign papers when I purchased land."

"Do not discount your husband's influence." He grimaced. "I worry that the world will come apart in his absence. Germans *trusted* him. I believe that dreadful war could have been avoided. No, I think you should scale back your activities. Widows do not run businesses. It is not done."

She put a hand on her hip. "No, no, no! Widows need income. I must feed my children. If I sit at home, we shall all starve."

"Do not discount the memory of the people of Wittenberg, dear cousin," he said with a frown. "They would not allow you to starve."

"Frau Luther! Frau Luther!"

Katie turned to see a former servant, Hilda approach. "Dearest Hilda, it is good to see you. Do you remember Doctor Ratzenberger?"

"Indeed I do! Good day, sir!" She ran toward Katie and curtsied to the doctor.

"Matthew, this is Hilda. I took her in as an orphan and trained her to work for me. And she can get more done in a day than the average woman."

"Ah! Good day! I seem to remember your face," he said, squinting. He turned back to his cousin. "Katie, I must see to my patients. We will talk again anon."

"Goodbye, Matthew." She turned to Hilda. "My dear, how are you? When did you return?"

"I came back with the Cranachs in the spring." The Cranachs and Luthers had been good friends for years. Lucas Cranach had painted an altar piece to her husband's specifications and painted portraits of both Katie and her husband. His wife, Barbara, had offered to take Hilda when Katie left. Barbara knew Katie would have all her children to provide for during the war.

A big smile spread over Katie's face. "I am just so glad that you are safe! Do you want your old job back? I intend to have boarders and sell beer again."

Hilda's gray-green eyes widened. "Frau Luther! Are you sure you want to do that without the good doctor?"

Katie's eyebrows shot up. "Why not?"

Hilda shuddered, and her fair skin seemed to get paler. "You did not see what happened after Easter. I did, and it gave me a turn."

Katie raised her eyebrows. "What happened?"

She leaned toward Katie and told her story in a hoarse whisper. "The Protestants lost Wittenberg, and Charles V rode into town—the very man who made Dr. Luther an outlaw. The old pig was puffed up with pride. Folk said he wanted to dig up Doctor Luther and hang him in the square, not that he did. The good doctor rests in his grave untouched. Duke Maurice signed an agreement with him in order to rule the province. Now he must obey a *Catholic.* None of us will be safe. And I hate to think what the emperor would do to Frau Luther. What would he do to your boarders?"

Sparks radiated from Katie's eyes, and she stamped her foot as she said, "I refuse to worry. I shall cling to my faith in Jesus and do what I must. I would like to see Charles the *thousandth* stop me."

Hilda blinked and looked shocked.

"Do you want a job?" Katie snapped.

"Y-Yes!"

"Then come with me." She grabbed Hilda's arm and began to walk. "I left the children to clean the Black Cloister and prepare the table for dinner."

An hour later, Katie left Hilda in the kitchen with cheese, cider, bread, sausage, and other provisions. She went in search of the children.

She found Margarete, who was thirteen, dusting a bedroom on the third floor. Margarete had her mother's red hair, heart-shaped face, and determined temperament. "Margarete, how did it go this morning?"

Her daughter ran a hand over her forehead and took a deep breath. "All the rooms are dusty, but nothing sustained damaged."

Katie nodded. *Maybe I can advertise for boarders right away.* "Your father's friend, Wolf Siebold, agreed to keep an eye on things. He must have done well. How much did the boys get done?"

Margarete waved her hand toward the door. "The boys got nothing done. Paul insisted on dusting all of Father's books. Martin wanted to play marbles, and Johann is entertaining friends."

Her mother chuckled. "Leave it to Paul to choose books. Well, it is time for dinner, so I shall get them organized."

Katie called all her children to dinner, and as they sat around the table, she talked about what they must do.

"I hoped that you boys would work with your sister to get the house in better shape."

Martin, who was sixteen, gestured toward his sister. "But Mother, she is just too bossy."

"I needed to study," said Johann, who was twenty-one. "My tutor promised to drill me on metaphysics this week."

"I understand your plans for study came to nothing," Katie said with raised eyebrows.

Johann frowned at his sister. "Visitors came, and Papa always told us to entertain strangers. I must not disobey Father!"

Fourteen-year-old Paul spoke up, "Papa's books are quite clean now and ready for anyone who needs to study."

"Very good, Paul." She turned to Martin. "Now Martin, you take the first floor. Sweep and air each room. I want you done before supper tonight."

"But—"

She held up her hand. "No excuses! Now, Johann, I want you to do the same to the second floor."

"My tutor will not—"

"Get it done quickly. In fact, I will isolate you in your room with your books afterward. I feel sure your father would approve."

"Paul, finish the third floor."

"Yes, Mama!"

"What about Margarete?" Martin whined.

"Margarete and I will look over the basement to see what provisions remain. Paul, join us there when you finish the third floor."

At that moment, Hilda appeared at the door. "Excuse me, ma'am. Your brother just arrived."

Katie pushed back her stool and ran around the table to embrace her brother. "Hans!"

Hans had thick, wavy brown hair with a tiny streak of gray at each temple. His tall, lanky frame swallowed his sister in a warm embrace. "Katie, I am so glad you could return in safety."

She pulled away from his arms and waved him to the table. "There should be another stool under the table, brother."

"Ach! I must embrace each of the children," he said as he went round to give each a hug and kiss.

At last Hans found a stool and sat down, after accepting a wooden plate from Hilda.

Katie returned to her place and sat down. "You spoke of my safe return, brother. I am not so sure that I am safe."

A frown creased his clean-shaven, oblong face. "What do you mean?"

"I want to re-establish our boarding house and sell beer," she said, frowning. "Today I met two of my four guardians. If I obey them, I shall be able to do nothing."

He reached for a slice of cheese. "Dear sister, remember I act as one of your guardians too. Tell me what they said."

She ticked off their opinions on her fingers. "Jacob does not want me to have a boarding house, but he wants me to sell beer. Matthew thinks I should not sell beer, but he wants me to have boarders—in a smaller house. Both of them fear I am unable to manage without masculine oversight. I have not even seen the town mayor. He shares the burden of my care too. How can I get anything done?"

A mischievous smile crept over her brother's face. "Well, you did not ask me if you should come back. So, I say you should not even be here."

Katie let out a tiny yelp and reached across the table to slap her brother's hand playfully. "I will take off a layer of hide."

Hans winced and looked meek. "Aye, she could do it too, children! You must do what she says."

"Hans, I am serious!" Katie shook her head. "Doctor Luther did not intend me to have guardians. And he wanted me to be in charge of the children. I have not even spoken to the children's guardians. I shall spend all my time meeting with men who want to guide me. What am I to do? I need no guidance."

As Katie finished her speech, Hans choked on his cider.

For a moment she could not tell if he was choking or laughing. "Hans? Hans? Are you all right?" She rushed around the table to pound his back.

"I-I...am...fine!"

Katie stopped pounding on his back. "Hans, are you laughing?"

He nodded.

She rolled her eyes, but when she looked at the children, she saw their eyes glued to her face. A smile tugged at Johann's face. Paul's face looked frozen as if he worried about being scolded for smiling. Margarete had her hand over her mouth as if holding in her laughter. Martin had his lips pressed together tightly. "Is everyone finished eating?"

No one spoke, but Hans continued coughing between chuckles.

"Children, go! You all have work to do. Hans and I must talk."

Without a word, her offspring fled, and she sank down on a stool beside Hans and waited for him to recover.

He rubbed his huge hands over his face. "Ach! That is much better. I can breathe again."

"What is the joke?" Katie said with raised eyebrows.

He took her small hand in his large one. "Sister, you must see the humor. You are complaining about not having freedom. Yet you have more freedom as a widow than any woman in Germany."

She bowed her head and looked at the floor a long time. In a tiny voice she said, "How do other widows survive?"

"Many of them are destitute. Some live with their families. Because you are Katie *Luther,* you can have a farm and sell beer."

"My husband would deplore the status of widows." She grimaced. "He thought women should be educated so they could provide for themselves."

Hans let go of her hand and tapped the table for emphasis. "Your husband changed the world. But a lot more needs to be done."

Tears sprang to her eyes. "I wish he were still here. The world needs him."

"Katie, think about what you said. *God* took him home."

She shook her head while she wiped away tears. "I know! That was a mistake. I *feel* like the world needs him."

Hans put his arm around her. "Your husband did so much. He gave us back Scripture in our language and a relationship with God. His job is completed. Now you are alone and must depend on Jesus."

She sniffled. "I do!"

"I have an idea." Hans said with a grin. "I could gather all of your guardians together. Maybe with all of them in one room, I could convince them of what you want to do."

"Oh, that would help." Her eyes lit up. "While you work on getting them together, I will go to all three of the farms and get them back in shape. I think Hilda can settle any boarders that might come while I am gone. Once I advertise for renters, I should get plenty of interest."

"Oh, Katie," Hans said, chuckling. "I shall have a bigger job than you."

"Why?" She shrugged.

"Because I shall have to plead for permission when I know you will have the jobs already completed. I *have* to succeed."

She looked into his dark eyes and chuckled.

Two months later, Katie carried a bouquet of fall flowers into the castle church. She walked slowly toward the front and stopped at the stone that marked her husband's grave. Red, blue, and yellow light filtered from the stained glass windows over the grave at her feet. "Doctor Luther, I miss you. You left instructions that I should have no guardians, but no one obeyed your wishes. I have lots of guardians, and I have to consult with two other men who oversee the children. I pray a lot. With the help of God, I have ten boarders now, and I am selling beer again in the town square. Two destitute girls just came, and I gave them jobs. I need to take out a loan to renovate the Black Cloister, and my guardians are in a quandary. But I have food and clothing, and so do the children. Someday I shall meet you again in heaven. Until then, I know God will help me to achieve whatever the family needs. I love you."

She placed the flowers on his grave and went back into the fall sunshine tearful, yet smiling.

# CHAPTER 9

# *Frenzied Flight*

Candlelight cast eerie shadows over the sumptuous furnishings as Richard Bertie walked into the darkened library. "Dearest Cathy, we have a summons."

The color left Cathy's face as she gasped and dropped her quill, splattering ink on the paper before her. "What?"

He crossed the thick woolen rug as he walked toward her. In his hand he held a paper made of parchment. "This just came from Stephen Gardiner. He called us to meet with him."

Her hands shook as she pushed her chair away from the engraved walnut desk. "Wh-Wh-What does it say?"

He pursed his lips as he pulled up an ornate chair to sit by her. "It bears the seal of the Crown, and it demands we present ourselves at the palace before the Lord Chancellor, Stephen Gardiner."

Since the sun had set, no light filtered through the multi-paned window to her right. So she took the paper from him and leaned toward the candelabrum on her desk. Her eyes narrowed as she read.

Catherine, Duchess of Suffolk, was thirty-four years old and quite pretty. She had toffee-brown hair, pale blue eyes, high cheek bones, and a flawless ivory complexion. Her mother had been a lady-in-waiting to

Queen Katherine of Aragon and her father an English courtier. Since her late husband, Charles Brandon, had been close to Henry VIII, Catherine had spent much of her life at court. Wealthy from her first husband's estate, she wore an embroidered gold dress. The snug bodice had a square neck. The sleeves were narrow at the shoulders, but they ballooned at the elbow and fastened at the wrist.

Wrinkling her nose, she tossed the paper toward her husband. "This is exceedingly wicked. That man is evil."

He leaned over to pick up the paper, which had landed on the floor beside her voluminous skirt. Her second husband, Bertie, had completed a degree at Cambridge and could read several languages. Before her first husband died, he hired Bertie to manage their affairs. Once the Duke of Suffolk died, Catherine sought Bertie's excellent judgment while she settled her husband's estate. While not considered handsome, his deportment suggested a cultured, intelligent man. He had receding brown hair, a full beard flecked with gray, large gray-green eyes, and full lips, which he often pressed together when thinking.

He cleared his throat. "I have been expecting this."

She scooted her chair closer to his and took his hand. "Aye! They imprisoned Hugh Latimer over a fortnight ago. At that time, I knew we could be next." A theologian and reformer, Latimer had preached often at court during the reign of Henry VIII. His sermons deplored the authority of the pope and clergy and pointed his listeners to the sacrifice of Christ. Catherine had heard him speak and put her faith in Christ. Afterward, she acquired a copy of Scripture in English. Along with the late Queen Kateryn Parr, she participated in Bible studies.

While still at Cambridge, Bertie found Christ, and their faith served as a deep bond. Many evenings they spent hours discussing the Bible and considering how to live by faith. As a result of their discussions, Catherine had furnished money to publish Protestant theologians, and supported needy ministers.

Bertie wore a frown as he took his wife's hand in both of his. "Queen Mary is determined to make England Catholic again." Mary, eldest daughter of Henry VIII, had just ascended to the throne. She took immediate steps to reverse her father's religious reforms and return England to Catholicism. Her priests began executing those who disagreed.

"Aye!" Cathy frowned and shook her head. "Henry disowned her when he divorced her mother. I daresay she wants revenge for what her mother suffered."

"Revenge must be left in the hands of God," Bertie said with a trembling voice. "But she must use force to accomplish her goals, because her beliefs cannot stand up under debate. Torture is a poor way to alter someone's opinion."

Cathy's eyebrows flew up. "My opinion shall not be changed."

Bertie groaned. "I know, my dear. But your distaste for Stephen Gardiner could have been a bit less obvious."

His wife pulled her hand from his. "What do you mean?"

He pursed his lips a moment then said, "The dog—I am sure you could have contrived another name for the dog."

She sniffed. "I rather think the name Gardiner is a suitable one for a dog. The man himself fails to act human most of the time. He plots and schemes to snatch the truth from the people and return us to popery. My dog actually behaves more like a human than he."

He spread his hands. "I agree about Gardiner, but perhaps a less personal attack on him would have been better. But then we had no idea he would return to power after Henry VIII died. Now we must think of a plan—we may be in mortal danger."

"Darling husband, we would still be in danger even if I named the dog John. We are Protestant. And Gardiner hates us."

Bertie frowned as he ran a trembling hand over his beard. "Aye, Gardiner hates us. He longs to purge the country of Protestants. He is dangerous!"

She bit her lip. "Aye, the man will burn us at the stake."

Her eyes wandered to their copy of the Great Bible, which lay on a huge pedestal table in the center of the room. Their chaplain used it for services, but they often read it together in the evenings. "Our faith is the core of our lives, and we must not waver. Just think—I could never have married you as a Catholic. Church leaders stopped relying on God's word, so they valued a person's status in life."

Her husband nodded.

"I would have married beneath my station, and authorities would have forbidden it. But as a Protestant, we study Scripture and believe each person is valuable in the eyes of God. Marriage to a believer is our only restriction. Can you imagine how much joy we would have missed?"

"I agree with you, dear wife. Much joy comes from obeying the truth, and we have been so happy together. We must not deny our faith. But what shall we do?" He punched his right fist into his left hand.

"I cannot help but think of Queen Kateryn Parr. How much Mary loved her. I wonder if the queen—had she lived—would be able to soften Mary now?"

He grimaced and shook his head. "Nay, Mary is adamant. Her mother received evil from Henry VIII, and she wants to restore her mother's church."

She threw up her hands. "Then what? We must also remember the baby. Whatever we do, we must find a way to protect her from popery." Cathy and Bertie had an infant daughter named Susan.

Anxiety twisted his face. He got up and paced the length of the room.

She extended trembling hands to him. "Dearest, come! We must pray for guidance."

In the semi-darkness, Cathy adjusted her full skirt as she knelt by the desk. Her husband, who wore tight hose, pantaloons, and a doublet that extended below his waist, waited until she settled herself and then knelt beside her. They joined hands and bowed their heads.

"Father, our lives are in danger. Please give us wisdom," Bertie prayed.

Cathy's heart fluttered as the red-uniformed soldier opened the door. She and her husband had traveled from their country estate in Lincolnshire to Barbican Manor, their home outside London. They had been waiting in St. James Palace to see Stephen Gardiner.

"The Lord Chancellor will see you now."

She glanced at Bertie. A muscle twitched in his jaw, but otherwise, his face wore a mask of calmness. Together they rose and entered his office.

Gardiner sat behind a massive desk inlaid with oak and walnut. Two carved wainscot chairs sat in front of his paper-cluttered desk. Sun streamed through huge bay windows across from his desk, making the room almost too warm. A uniformed page hovered at his elbow with a stack of papers. An ordained priest, the Lord Chancellor wore a clerical robe—a full white gown gathered into a yoke below the neck, over a dark undershirt. His long beard and thinning hair made his oblong face look almost square.

"You came at last. I expected you yesterday." His drooping eyelids made him look very sleepy.

Bertie bowed. "My lord, your summons arrived at dusk. The trip from Lincolnshire is about eighty miles. We made haste and arrived late last night."

The Lord Chancellor opened his lids wide, and Catherine could see his small, dark eyes. "Nay, that cannot be true. I sent the summons at noon two days ago."

Hands clasped behind his back, Bertie kept his eyes on Gardiner's face. "Indeed, my lord, my servant will testify to the time. And your lordship must allow ample travel time."

Gardiner threw up his arms, and his long, loose sleeves slid to his armpits, leaving his thin wrinkled arms exposed. "Aye, I dare say your servant will parrot anything you say. But my business is about a loan. My records indicate your wife's late husband, Duke of Suffolk, owed Henry VIII a sum of money. I wish to collect that debt now."

Bertie lifted his chin and moved closer to the desk. "Perhaps you should recheck your records. When the Duke died, the judge instructed the executor to make regular payments. We have done that, and at present, only two payments remain. I know Her Majesty would not violate the law."

A frown creased the old man's face, and his eyes disappeared amongst his wrinkles. "That can be verified, however, Her Majesty, Queen Mary, has the right to demand payment of any outstanding loan when she comes to the throne."

Bertie closed his eyes a moment before he spoke. "Aye, with only two payments left, I feel sure we could accommodate the Queen."

Catherine's face flushed as Gardiner's eyes went up and down her dress. That day, she had chosen not to wear a court dress. Her dress of royal blue had a full skirt, the high neck and full sleeves bordered by Italian lace—not high fashion. *He is trying to guess the value of my dress. I was right to wear one of my least expensive. The nave wants our money.*

"Excellent! There is, however, another matter which is weightier," Gardiner said. The wrinkles on his face seemed to quiver.

At that pronouncement, the duchess felt a pang in her stomach. *Is this the moment?*

"Aye? And what is that?" Bertie had moved away from the desk as if the interview was almost over.

"I need to ensure that your chaplain has changed your family communion back to the traditional form. With all the heretics in prison, it should be easier to revert to Catholic traditions." The loose skin over his eyes tightened, revealing his smoldering dark eyes.

Bertie's face went white. "We have made no changes to our worship service."

Gardiner's face reddened and swelled so that the wrinkles seemed less noticeable. "That must be done right away. You will have read the decree by the queen. Catholic doctrine and traditions are now restored. Each church in England must comply."

Her husband gazed at Gardiner with a passive face, but she saw his hands balled into fists behind his back. "I did hear of the queen's decree."

The Lord Chancellor pounded his desk with a thin, claw-like fist. "That is good news, and I feel sure you will obey, since the consequences could be unpleasant." He turned his face toward Catherine. "Duchess, how is your dog?"

She curtsied, sucked in her breath, and tried to keep her face calm. Despite her efforts, her left cheek wanted to twitch, and she hoped she did not look angry. She controlled her voice and repeated the phrase she had practiced before her mirror. "Thank you, sir. My little dog is well. He is the best natured dog—"

"I have a request, sir," Bertie interrupted.

"A request?" Every wrinkle on Gardiner's face seemed to frown.

"The Spanish royal family owes the duchess money." He nodded toward his wife. "I would like to request permission to go to the continent to retire the debt."

Gardiner started shaking his head, but he paused and raised his gray eyebrows. "Is this a large debt?"

Catherine thought she could see his eyes flash beneath the heavy lids. *If we bring money into England, he could seize it all if he arrests us.*

Her husband shrugged. "Aye. And we have tried every method possible to retrieve the money. I must do it in person."

The sagging skin around his mouth curled into a smile. "I shall have my secretary prepare a pass for you. The duchess must stay here, of course."

"Thank you, sir!" Bertie bowed and turned to leave.

"A moment!" Gardiner said. His wrinkles looked frozen in place. "I must know how to contact you."

"We are staying at Barbican Manor, just outside London." He grabbed his wife's arm, and they left the room.

She breathed a sigh of relief once they left the building. "I thought he would refuse you."

Bertie stopped in front of their carriage. A servant opened the door, and he helped her inside.

She took her husband's hand and squeezed. "Our plan worked."

"Quietly, dearest," he whispered. "Once I am in Europe, I can find a safe place for us. Then I shall send word for you to come. You *should* be safe at Barbican Manor while I am gone."

A tear trickled down Cathy's face, and she brushed it away. Her restless hands fingered the long string of pearls that hung down the front of her red silk gown. She stood looking out the sitting room window. Snow flakes drifted down from the sky like cotton and rested on the bare limbs of the trees. Robins walked across the snow of the landscape. A well-bundled servant trudged past, but she saw no one else. *Bertie has been gone for six months. I have heard nothing. Dear God, help me not to worry. Keep him safe.*

The housekeeper knocked and then entered the room with a pinched look on her face. "Duchess, a tradesman insists on speaking to you. I tried to send him away, but he would not go. Shall I call the sheriff?"

The duchess turned, and her eyes gleamed. "Did he give you a name?"

The housekeeper frowned and closed her eyes. "I paid no attention, but it started with a 'c.' Was it Craddock? No, Conwell."

"Aye, that is the man." Her heart leapt for joy, but she willed her face to display a placid reaction. "The Duchess of Sussex promised to send a salesman who could obtain a rare type of silk. Send him up."

The housekeeper grimaced a little and then left the room with a curtsey.

Moments later she returned with an elderly man. "Madam, this is George Conwell."

Once the door closed, the elderly man stepped forward. He had short gray hair, a rounded face, and a long, crooked nose. His eyebrows went up, and his dark blue eyes looked at her with a question.

"One moment!" She tiptoed to the door and glanced up and down the hall with a secretive look on her face. "Aye, we are alone now. Do you have news from Bertie?"

He pulled a sealed paper from his jacket and placed it in her hand. "I do. He gave me instructions. It must be burned after reading."

She broke the seal with eagerness, unfolded the paper, and read it several times. "Dearest Bertie, it is so good to see your hand writing again." *This is my summons. He said to be careful whom I trust. My flight must be secret.*

The older man watched while she read.

At last she tucked the paper in her skirt and looked up. Her face wore an eager smile. "When do you think I should leave?"

He waved a thin hand. "We must be gone tonight."

She sucked in her breath. "But I must make plans, gather clothes. And there is the baby to consider."

He leaned closer to her and handed her a map. "I believe your life is in danger. Choose two or three servants you trust. You should plan to leave just after dark and meet me at Broken Wharf. I shall have a small boat to take you down the Thames."

The duchess looked at the map for a moment. After cramming the map into her pocket, she sank onto the couch and cradled her head in her hands. "This is so sudden. What do you suspect?"

He raised his scraggy white eyebrows. "You have a spy, maybe even two, amongst the servants."

A shudder ran down her spine. "How do I know whom to trust?"

"I would not trust anyone who tends to be too curious about your activities or that you have not known for years."

She closed her eyes and nodded. "That describes my housekeeper. She watches me closely."

He extended his hand to her. "Your husband entrusted your safety to me. Be very careful."

With a grimace, she pulled the letter from her pocket and kissed it. "I must burn this," she said, as she tossed his letter in the fireplace.

Cathy, trying not to make a sound, hovered in the evergreen trees midway between the house and the road. Since the sun set early in winter, she left the house just after nine. Conwell arranged their departure so they would catch the tide going out the Thames, and she gave herself plenty of time to find him at the river. While slipping through the yard, she had heard an ominous sound. Her eyes peered into the blackness. *If I could only see.*

The maid, Maria, who held her baby, whispered, "Madam—"

"Sh-Sh-Sh! If we are caught now, they will arrest us."

A whimper. "Dearest Susan, you must be silent," the duchess whispered as she patted the bundle that Maria held.

Moments seemed like hours, and her heart pounded with such intensity that she feared it would betray their position. *Precious Savior, help me!*

After waiting for awhile and straining her ears, she squared her shoulders and leaned toward Maria's ear. "Follow me! Quietly!"

The two ladies crept across the yard to the gate, which a faithful servant had left unlocked. Just as they stepped outside the gate, a voice sounded, "Who goes there?"

"Quick!" Cathy grabbed Maria's arm and pulled her into the road just as light flooded the yard.

"Hello?"

Catherine led Maria into thick evergreen shrubbery by the road. Footsteps sounded in the fenced yard they had just left.

"Mama!"

"Sh-Sh!" Catherine's mouth felt like cotton, and her skin was icy despite her heavy cloak. She could feel Maria's breath on her neck and smell the pine scent of the shrub.

"Madam, I dropped the bundle of Susan's clothes—just inside the gate," Maria whispered. "Should I fetch them?"

"No!" The duchess felt her stomach lurch. "We will stay here until they walk back to the house with the lantern."

The moments ticked away—each one lasted twice as long as it should. The wind moaned through the trees, and she gritted her teeth to keep them from chattering. At last the light faded, and the sound of footsteps died away.

She put a trembling hand on Maria's arm. "Now come with me."

Catherine and Maria tiptoed out of the shrubbery and down the road toward the wall that surrounded London. Conwell had given her detailed instructions on a way to enter the wall after the guard closed the gates.

"There is a doorway. He promised to ensure it remained open for us." The duchess led her maid up to the heavy oak door set into the stone wall. She pushed with all her might.

*E-E-E-E-EK!* The hinges creaked as the door opened a crack.

Cathy cringed and glanced around her to see if the noise had brought the guards. "Hurry, Maria. We must get inside and into the darkness."

The two ladies scurried inside the narrow opening, and Catherine found a dark corner in which to hide. Pressed against the icy stone wall of a nearby building, Catherine, every nerve tense, listened for someone to respond to the noise. Her heart fluttered as she caught her breath. *Please give us safety, dear Father.*

"Milady, should we close the door?" Maria said into her ear.

"No!"

"Mama." Susan poked her head out of the blankets and held out her arms.

She took the baby and cuddled her for a moment. "Little Susan, you have been so sweet. But you must be quiet. Maria, please take her. I must consult the map."

Maria took the baby and bundled the blanket around her again while the duchess stepped out of the shadows to examine the map Conwell had drawn.

*I hope the street names are visible.* She stepped out into the cobblestone street and made her way to the river. Every few feet the duchess stepped into the darker shadows along the roadside to listen. Only when she felt certain did she move back into the roadway.

"Madam, how far is the river now?" Maria whispered as they huddled together in a darkened alley.

"I fear I have lost my way. We have gone by Silver Street twice now." She knew she must head south to find the Thames, but fog made it hard to see. "I wish I could see the North Star."

Crash!

Catherine covered her mouth to hold back a scream.

"Wh-What was th-that?" Maria asked.

"Sh!" Her chest tightened, but she closed her eyes and breathed a silent prayer. When she opened her eyes, she saw the reason for the noise—a chunk of ice just beyond her feet lay on the cobblestone. The wind had blown it out of the trees.

Another gust of wind blew snow into their faces, and the icy wind cut through their warm clothes. Baby Susan whimpered.

"Quiet, little one. Your mama will get us to safety," Maria whispered.

Catherine stepped into the light to check the map once again. "We are a few feet behind the churchyard. I hope Sally and Frederick have arrived." She had instructed Sally and Frederick, both lifetime servants, to meet them at the river.

An icy breeze swept along the dark street, and both ladies shivered. "Milady, how much further?"

"This is the last stretch." Catherine consulted the map. "I thought we were lost. We must cross the cemetery, so watch for gravestones."

The two ladies crept through the churchyard as silently as possible. Catherine almost twisted her ankle in a small depression, but she caught herself and trudged on. She and Maria crossed the street as they headed toward the river.

"Duchess?"

Catherine jumped at the sudden masculine voice, but saw the faint outline of a man emerge from the fog. "Yes? Who are you?"

"Conwell. We must hurry. Come!"

"B-B-But sir, a man and woman were to meet me here."

"Fredrick and Sally arrived. The sailboat is here." He led them to a pier and a narrow sailboat built for travel in the Thames. He helped them aboard.

She thought she could make out the dark image of a man on deck, but the sails obstructed her view. "Where is the crew?"

"Aye, they are here," he said, waving toward the deck. "Follow me to the hull. Then we can be off."

Catherine and Maria entered an oblong room, where she saw dark shapes on the floor.

A male voice whispered. "Duchess, is that you?"

"Yes. Who are you?" Cathy said.

"I am Frederick. My wife, Sally, is here too."

Tears stung Catherine's eyes. "Did you bring your bundles?"

"Yes!" Frederick answered. "I have a small bag of food, and Sally has some clothing."

"Madam, lie here beside me," Sally said. "I have several blankets on the floor."

Maria and the duchess settled themselves and the baby on the floor. Soon the ship began to move. The gentle motion relaxed the duchess, and she soon fell asleep.

A soft hand touched her face, and Catherine sat up. The morning light, muted by fog, filtered across the hull through a small round window. Susan, her dark hair rumpled, smiled into her face. "Mama?"

"Sh! The others will wake." On the dirty floor, her three servants slept under dark brown blankets. The boat swayed, but it no longer moved forward.

Susan's chubby face puckered into a frown. "Waaaaaah!"

"Sh!" The duchess gathered the child in her arms.

The hull door opened, and Mr. Conwell entered. He threw back the hood of his heavy black cloak. The wrinkles on his face seemed deeper, and his eyes looked tired. "Keep the baby quiet, if you can. We moved rapidly last night and arrived at a city called Leigh on the Sea. Last night we could hear a ship behind us and worried we were followed."

Catherine winced, and a shiver ran through her body. "Maria dropped a bundle of Susan's clothes. If they missed me and found the clothes, they might be looking for us."

His already-fair skin blanched as he grimaced. "Then we must assume you are in danger, and pray you are not. I went ashore. I overheard the authorities, and they are searching for someone."

A pain shot through her abdomen. "No! What should we do?"

"I have a plan. How are you dressed?" His dark blue eyes peered at the rough woolen cloak she wore.

Still holding Susan, she glanced down at her cloak. "Under this cloak I have on a simple blouse, vest, and skirt I purchased for my maid."

He nodded. "Excellent! But you must also change your demeanor. Instead of your usual confident style, you must keep your eyes downcast. The common woman appears demure and meek. Speak only when someone speaks to you, and do not make eye contact."

"Like this?" She bowed her head and assumed a look of passivity.

"Good! You will be Mrs. Fitch, and you are here to visit your father, Clive Smith. He has a married daughter, and he owns a local pub. You will stay there today. Tonight Bertie should arrive, and we will cross the channel to Europe."

"B-B-But what if someone knows his daughter?"

He crossed his arms and shook his head. "She has never visited here. You should be safe if he identifies you."

She sighed and hugged Susan tighter. "May God protect us!"

Susan whined.

Catherine glanced down at Susan, who sucked her fingers while she whimpered. "I think Susan is hungry. The servants have food, but I do not wish to wake them."

He pulled back his cloak and unfastened a cloth sack attached to his belt. The bag held a small loaf of bread. "Here, this should work for now. We will go ashore soon, Mrs. Fitch."

With clammy hands, she reached for the bread. "Thank you! Thank you!"

The acrid taste of vomit lingered in her mouth. She had thrown up several times now, yet her stomach still churned. Their ship ran into a storm, and the wild lurching of the ship had been too much for her. She lay, eyes closed, in the captain's cabin, on a thin mattress stuffed with straw. The wind and waves lashed the ship, rocking it back and forth. She was thankful the captain had his bed secured to the floor. Bertie had arrived in Leigh on the Sea, and their trip across the channel had begun just after dark.

A door opened, and she heard a voice. "Dearest?"

She tried to rise onto her elbow, but felt another wave of nausea.

Her husband staggered with the lurching of the boat as he made his way to her bed. "The captain is worried, dearest."

She swallowed hard before she answered. "Worried?"

"The wind is blowing us back toward England."

The duchess winced. "God help us!"

Her husband now stood over her bed, hanging onto the rafters to keep his balance. The boat creaked and moaned as the waves dashed against its sides. A deep frown creased his brow. "Dearest, I constructed a plan to outsmart Gardiner. And Conwell concocted a way to avoid officials in Leigh. I managed to arrive at Leigh undetected, and we both used our wits to get aboard a ship leaving England. But I cannot devise a plan for this storm."

She frowned, took his hand, and squeezed hard. "Going back to England now will be fatal."

"Yes! The queen will execute us both." A grimace twisted his face, and the veins stood out in his throat. "We must pray, dearest. God alone can help us now."

He sat on her bed and took her hands in his.

"Almighty Father, we sought your face, and you guided us. Using our minds we devised a way around all obstacles. But we can do no more. Death holds no terror for us," Bertie prayed. "We would be in your presence because of our faith in Christ. But we ask for you to protect us from the injustice of Queen Mary."

"Precious Father, we acknowledge that we are made of dust. You have the power to take life or save it. I have no power over storms, but you do. Convey us safely to Europe. And give us comfort in this storm," Catherine prayed. "Help us to further the cause of your kingdom. We rely on your wisdom and protection."

She opened her eyes and wiped tears from her face. Her husband did the same.

"I brought a copy of the Scriptures. Let me read to you."

She lay back again on the bed, and he sat down beside her, and read.

Two hours later, a knock sounded on the door.

Bertie stopped reading and called, "Come in."

Conwell stood in the door. His rounded face wore a smile, and his blue eyes danced. "The captain said the storm is subsiding, and the wind is shifting. We can now see the continent, and we will land in less than an hour.

A radiant smile broke over Bertie's face, and he kissed his wife.

"Praise the Lord," Catherine said.

"Amen!"

# CHAPTER 10

# A Better Man

"Ouch!" Susannah said, but no one heard her in the shoving crowd. Someone had poked her hard in the ribs. Men, dressed in waistcoats and bowties, accompanied by ladies in long, sweeping skirts, surged into the building. Their eyes had anxious expressions, and their faces wore frowns. She looked around to see who had been so rude, but she could not tell. No one looked embarrassed or even met her eye. Tension swept through the masses. Grunting and murmuring, they elbowed each other to get to the doors.

She and her fiancé, Charles Haddon Spurgeon, stood just inside the doorway of a public building in downtown London. On the second floor, Spurgeon would preach an early evening sermon in a public lecture room. Light from gas chandeliers overhead mingled with the rays of the setting sun streaming in from outside. The foyer doors stood open behind her, and a fall breeze rustled the ladies' bonnets while whisking amongst the bare-headed men.

"We have to go up those stairs," Charles whispered in her ear as he guided her through the throng. He held his top hat under his right arm and nodded toward the stairway ahead.

She leaned over to ask a question, but at that moment, his head was turned away while he greeted a man on the opposite side. *Dearest Charles is so gracious.*

Charles Haddon Spurgeon had accepted the pastorate of London's Park Street Chapel in 1854. News of his excellent sermons spread throughout the city, and people mobbed any church where he preached. Hundreds professed faith in Christ because of his ministry. Now, a year later, he had agreed to a midweek sermon at a large London lecture hall. Spurgeon and Susannah planned to marry in a few months, and he had asked her to accompany him to the service.

Susannah, daughter of a well-to-do family, had a fierce loyalty for her fiancé. Despite her shyness, she had worked for weeks to raise a hundred pounds toward the new auditorium her church planned to build for him. In addition, she had made her mother stop taking *The Ipswich Express,* a local newspaper, because the editor criticized Spurgeon and his sermons. Earlier today, she had deliberated for hours about the perfect dress for this evening's service. As his future wife, she wanted to leave the right impression. She wore a floor length dress of beige wool. Each tier of her flounced skirt had an ornate border of blue flowers. Since the weather had turned cool, she also wore a baby blue shawl and bonnet to match. Her light brown hair hung in ringlets, framing an elegant face with high cheekbones. Her eyes resembled the color of the sky on a cloudless day. A grimace, however, creased her pretty face. *These people act like barbarians.* Her parents gave her a proper education, and she knew etiquette. This crowd was bereft of manners.

At last the couple reached the steps and with difficulty began to ascend the floral carpeted stairs. Susannah felt dizzy as people pressed in front and behind her. They had entered the stairwell on the left beside the hand rail. She reached out her left hand to grasp the engraved railing while she clutched her fiancé with the right. *I must not fall. These folk might trample on me.* Her fashionable beaded purse hung limply from her left wrist until the crowd pushed forward and it got caught in the vertical wood railings. She felt the drawstring tighten. Since the purse was a recent gift from her mother, she worried it might be damaged. She tried to pull it loose but had to release Spurgeon's arm. Once she secured her purse, she checked to see that it had sustained no damage. Afterward, she reached for her fiancé, but saw instead a lady in a green muslin dress beside her.

"Charles? Charles?" she screamed.

Up ahead she could just see the back of his straight, brown hair and dark overcoat. She eased up onto the next step and said, "Charles, I am back here."

But he moved further away.

*Surely he must know I am not with him.* "Charles!" Her stomach lurched as his head disappeared in the mob. *Where is he?*

For a moment the room spun, and her heart pounded. The crowd surged forward, and she eased up to the next step, but she felt lightheaded. *I am alone and can hardly breathe. Surely he will come back to escort me.*

She relied on sheer determination to struggle up to the landing. But once on level ground, the crowd pressed even tighter. She inched her way to the wall and leaned against the brocade wallpaper. The pungent smells of body odor and ladies' perfumes permeated the air. Perspiration broke out on her face, so she untied her shawl and draped it on her arm. She glanced at her gold watch, which hung from a broach pinned to her dress, and light from a sconce overhead glittered over the crystals embedded around its face. *The service does not commence for thirty-five minutes, and already the place is packed. Where is he? Does he miss me?*

Her eye caught a young couple on the edge of the crowd. The pretty lady, resplendent in a rose-colored gown with a burgundy shawl, clung to the man's arm, and her blue eyes twinkled as she talked to him. The man had his head turned toward his lady's face, and he lifted her gloved hand to his mouth, giving it a prolonged kiss as they moved forward toward the balcony door.

*How sweet! He is captivated.* She fingered her watch and stood on tiptoe, expecting to see Charles coming toward her. However, he did not appear. *Obviously, that man loves her, unlike Charles, who seems to be unaware I exist.*

Suddenly fear and frustration exploded into anger. Once again she checked the time, and she stamped her foot. *I do not intend to stand here and be crushed.*

With a firm set to her pretty jaw, she gathered up her full skirt and flung her body into the crowd. *I am going home!* "Excuse me! Pardon me! Sorry!"

Inch by inch she forced her way through the thickening crowd until she reached the ground floor again. Turning sideways and apologizing, she fought her way to the door. To her surprise, the throng of people extended to the cobblestone walkway outside. She did not get out of the crowd until she had gone several blocks down the road.

"Goodness! I am glad to be out of that!" As she inhaled the crisp fall breeze, she flung her head back, threw her shawl around her shoulders, and strutted down the walkway. *Reverend Spurgeon just lost one faithful follower—me!*

For a moment she paused and looked back at the crowds who were trying to enter the building. *Should I go back? He might worry, and I really did not wait that long.*

At that moment a man wearing a tattered gray shirt and baggy trousers bumped into her. Instead of apologizing, he brushed past her and hurried toward the auditorium. She turned on her heel and walked away. *My escort forgot me, and I shall go home before someone injures me.*

After she stalked a few more yards, she stopped to look inside her purse. *Do I have enough for a cab? Yes, I do!* With sufficient coins in her hand, she hung her purse back on her arm and moved to the street. Just ahead she spotted a cab stand with a vacant cab. She raised her hand and hailed the driver.

"2341 Monroe Street," she said with a triumphant gleam in her eye.

The driver nodded.

She climbed inside and collapsed against the upholstered cushions while the driver prodded the horse into the street. A frown on her brow, she watched the travelers fill the street. Horse drawn carriages, men on horseback, and wagons belonging to tradesman moved into the street around them. Now her cab inched along, even though she wanted to get home quickly. The evening rush had begun. Biting her lip, she sighed.

*I have been so loyal to him. It almost hurt to ask people for money, but I did it because I love Charles. And Mother argued with me about canceling the newspaper. She told me it was Father's favorite. Maybe Charles fails to love me as deeply as I love him. Mother entrusted me to him for the evening. With pickpockets and ruffians in downtown London, I could have been harmed. Besides, leaving me to find my own way was very rude. He should have seated me himself before the meeting started.*

After gazing at the street now clogged with travelers, she closed her eyes and let her mind go back to that afternoon. Charles came for her early and took her to a fashionable tea shop.

They settled into their comfortable chairs at the lace covered table beside a window with white lace curtains. Uniformed waitresses, who carried silver platters and china dishes, moved about the room which was adorned in dainty chintz wallpaper. As she removed her gloves, she pointed out an engraved silver vase on the table containing a pink rosebud.

"Charles, look at the rose."

"Exquisite!" he said. "But my love, your enchanting face surpasses any flower."

Susannah felt her face grow warm. She demurred while she adjusted the silverware. "I cannot compare myself to such a lovely flower."

He cocked one eyebrow. "I can, and I do. Not only are you beautiful, you are my friend, companion, and soon-to-be-wife. I am so thankful for you."

"Thank you, Charles. I am honored." She raised her eyes to his.

He reached over to touch her hand. "Susie, I love you!"

The blush on her fair complexion deepened. "Oh, Charles! I love you as well."

"We both know Christ, so I shall love you even in heaven. Nothing can tear my love from you—not even death."

She sighed as she gazed into his face.

With a jerk, the cab came to a halt in front of her house, and the memory faded.

"We have arrived, Madam."

Susannah stepped out of the carriage and handed the driver enough coins to cover her fare.

She stamped up the stairs to her front door. *Everlasting love indeed!*

After she entered the foyer, she slammed the door, rattling the glass ornaments in the hall curio cabinet. A maid appeared, and Susie tossed both shawl and bonnet toward her. She brushed past the palms that sat in the entrance hall and ran up the carpeted stairs to her room.

"Susie?" Her mother's voice came from behind her and sounded puzzled.

*Mama must be in the sitting room. But I do not wish to talk.* Without pausing, she darted to her bedroom, where she collapsed on her pink canopy bed. She caught a whiff of the rose potpourri which sat on her bedside table and thought of the rose in the tea shop.

"He said I was prettier than the rose on our table. But how could he love me at all?" she said. Tears sprang to her eyes, and she rolled over, plunging her face into her pillow.

"Susie?" The muffled sound of her mother's voice came through the closed door. "Susie, is something wrong?"

While she sniffled and brushed aside tears, Susannah dragged herself to her feet and opened the door.

Her mother saw her tearstained face and fluffed the curls on her forehead. "Susie? What happened? You are back much too early."

"We got separated, and he forgot me," she said. Sobs tore at her throat anew, and she threw herself into her mother's arms.

Like her daughter, Mrs. Thompson was an attractive woman. She had blue eyes and brown, wavy hair, now streaked with gray. Her forehead wrinkled in thought while she held Susannah in her arms.

Susie cried a long time and refused her mother's attempts to reassure her. Her tears did subside at last.

"Tell me what happened, Susie." The two ladies sat down in chairs upholstered in pink rosebuds by Susie's white French dressing table, and Mrs. Thompson handed her an embroidered handkerchief.

Susie took a deep breath and wiped her eyes. Her face was blotchy and her eyes red. "Charles took me to Marie's Tea Shop just off Piccadilly Circus. He was not anxious to linger once we finished our tea, so we headed toward the lecture hall. Throngs already crowded the building when we got there, and while going upstairs to the lecture hall, I lost him when I stopped to untangle my purse from the stair railings. I waited and waited, but he did not come back for me. Finally, I got a cab and came home."

Mrs. Thompson pursed her lips a moment. "He must have been intent on his sermon."

"Mama, how could he forget me?" Tears spilled down her face again. "Is it possible that he does not love me as much as I love him?"

"No, Susannah, I know he loves you." She squeezed her daughter's hand.

"Do you recall how hard it was for me to ask people for money?" Susie dabbed at the tears with her mother's handkerchief. "My heart pounded like it would leap from my body, but I did it for *him*."

"I know dearest, and he was quite touched," Mrs. Thompson said in a soothing tone.

She spread her arms and raised her voice. "Then how could he forget I exist and desert me in a crowded building? That was quite rude."

Her mother patted her knee. "Normally I would agree, but your future husband is a very *unusual* man."

"He would have to be unusual after making such lush professions of love." Susie rolled her eyes. "You should have heard him in the tea room. He said I was lovelier than any flower on earth."

"The power of God is on him in a special way, Susie." Mrs. Thompson said, raising her eyebrows. "His thoughts probably centered on reaching the lost."

"But what if something had happened to me?" Susie's eyes blazed. "London is filled with thugs. One of them could have attacked me."

Mrs. Thompson wagged a finger in her daughter's face. "You returned home in complete safety."

"And for that I shall thank myself." Susie raised her chin.

"I disagree." Mrs. Thompson shook her head. "God took care of you when Charles focused on his responsibility."

"But—Mama!" She crossed her arms and hugged herself. "I long for Charles to protect me."

"You must understand that his ministry is also his obsession."

Susie's mouth fell open. At last she whispered, "Obession?"

"Yes, Susie." Mrs. Thompson nodded. "He may not always be as attentive as you want."

"What?" Her blue eyes were wide, and a frown wrinkled her brow.

"Yes, my dear." Her mother's eyebrows rose. "I think you should know. He will be quite busy with his ministry."

Susie paused and took several deep breaths. "I saw a couple today on the balcony while I waited for Charles to come back. The man could hardly take his eyes off his lady. I always wished for someone to love me like that."

Mrs. Thompson made a clucking sound with her mouth, and then she said, "Dearest, *you are thinking of yourself.*"

Susie pressed her lips together and twisted her mother's handkerchief into a very tight knot.

Two hours later, Susannah, now relaxed, sat in her bedroom listening to her mother read poetry. Suddenly, a maid, dressed in a crisp, white uniform, knocked and then opened the door. "Excuse me." She curtsied. "Reverend Spurgeon is downstairs. He is quite distraught and is asking about Miss Thompson."

Susannah shrank back and turned her face away. "I have no wish to see him."

"I shall see him," Mrs. Thompson said, putting the book of poems aside. She rose. "Please take him to the sitting room."

The maid left, and Mrs. Thompson turned to her daughter. "He will want to speak to you. You cannot avoid it."

Susie shrugged and did not look her mother in the eye.

Mrs. Thompson left the room and shut the door with a determined click.

*I cannot face him. He would see how angry I am—what if he says it is a sin? Maybe mother will explain on my behalf. Will he apologize?* For a few moments she indulged in a fantasy where he begged for her forgiveness.

She gazed in the gilded mirror over her dressing table and straightened her hair. "I want him to be mesmerized with me."

Her mother's words echoed in her mind. *You are thinking of yourself.*

Mrs. Thompson knocked on the door and then came in. A pleading expression on her face, she gestured toward the door. "Dearest, come with me. Charles is waiting."

"I would rather not." She turned away.

"When he came in, he was quite distressed, and it took quite an effort to reassure him. Now he wants to speak to you."

Susie turned, and her eyes glittered as she said, "You say he was anxious? How did he respond when you explained?"

Her mother raised her eyebrows. "I merely assured him of your safety."

"You did not relate the incident?" She frowned. "*I* have to tell him?"

"Yes, come. He has been worried, and I promised you would come straight away!" Mrs. Thompson motioned toward the door.

Susie hung back. *Mama will be impossible if I do not give in, but I am terrified. He has never seen me upset.*

Mrs. Thompson took her arm. "Do come, dearest!"

*What shall I say? Will he scold me like Mama did?* Susannah followed. Her stomach churned, and her heart pounded as if she walked to her execution. At last, she reached the sitting room. When she entered, she saw him pacing in front of the velvet curtains. He wore the same navy suit as he had earlier in the day, but his shoulders sagged.

He came toward her with his hands extended. "Susie, thank God you are unhurt."

"Good evening, Reverend!" She did not meet his eye. Instead she curtsied and walked away from him to the camel back couch on the other side of the room. She settled herself on the burgundy brocade cushions. A carved mahogany table beside her held an oil lamp that sent flickering light across her lap. Avoiding her fiancé's eye, she arranged each tier of her flounced skirt.

Wearing a worried expression, Spurgeon walked toward her and stood beside a French arm chair on the right side of the couch. "May I sit?"

"Please do!" She glanced up for just a moment and returned to smoothing the floral decorations on her skirt.

He eased himself onto the edge of the fine upholstery, pulled out a handkerchief, and blotted his forehead. "I stepped down from the platform after I completed the sermon and closed the service. While I stood in the hallway behind the platform, I turned to ask you a question. Suddenly I realized I had not seen you since we entered the building. I waved aside the people who wanted to consult with me and asked the ushers to help search for you. We covered the entire building. When we finished and found no trace of you, I…I was frantic. I worried you had…come to some harm. P-Please tell me what happened."

*So he did miss me*—after *his sermon.* She looked into his face for the first time and noticed lines of fatigue around his mouth and eyes. His hair was mussed, as if he had run his fingers through it over and over, and his bowtie was askew. "I held onto your arm," she said, "until we reached the steps, but my purse caught in the railing. The crowd pushed forward, and you went on without me. I thought…I thought you… would come back for me, but you did not."

Spurgeon cringed and tugged at his collar. "So I lost you in the crowd *before* the service. I had no idea."

She sniffed, anger mounting, which strengthened her resolve. "Finally I made it up to the landing, but there the crowd packed in even more tightly. I moved to the wall, thinking you would return. I started wondering...how you could love me...and *completely* forget I existed."

He ran his fingers through his dark brown hair and winced. "Please go on."

"At this point I-I lost my temper." She gazed right into his eyes and said, "I *willingly* fought the crowd to get out of the building. Even outside, I had to *battle* people still trying to get in. I intended to walk, but fortunately, I could afford to hire a cab to take me home, which I did. Frankly, you displayed terrible manners. What did you expect me to do? Find my own seat? How *unspeakably* rude!"

Spurgeon pounded a fist on his thigh and shook his head. "I should have noticed—"

Mrs. Thompson, who had been hovering at the window, stepped forward and interrupted. "I reminded Susie that the Spirit of the Almighty is on you in a special way. His presence pushed aside earthly concerns. The sermon dominated your thoughts. She should not selfishly expect you to dote on her when spiritual issues are pressing. In fact, as your wife, she should never anticipate being coddled by one busy with *eternal* matters."

Spurgeon grimaced and ran a trembling hand over his mouth. "Mrs. Thompson, I respect and honor you, and it pains me to contradict you. But, I cannot allow you to blame the Spirit of God for my failure. Yes, madam, the Holy Spirit is on me. However, he would not lead me to endanger so sacred a trust. I was responsible for your daughter, and my actions were rude and inexcusable."

Susannah's eyes widened as she eyed her fiancé. *Mama gives him an excellent excuse, but he refuses exoneration. How noble.*

With a sigh, he scooted his chair closer and reached to take her hand. "Beloved, I failed you today, and I offer you my humblest apology. In spite of my actions, I do love you. Next to God, I love you more than anyone else in this world. Yet, I abandoned you. I wonder if I can even forgive myself. But I ask—even beg you. Will you forgive me, please?"

She gazed into the depths of his dark brown eyes, and her heart fluttered. *I imagined an apology of sorts, but he is far more humble than I could conceive. His face looks worn and tired. He is really upset.* She put her hand on top of his. "Oh, Charles, yes! I forgive you."

A smile spread across his face, and he pointed to the couch. "May I sit beside you?"

She nodded.

He rose and settled himself by her side, then he cleared his throat. Raising his eyebrows he said, "I have another question for you. Your mother brought up something we should discuss. Being married to me will not be easy."

She knitted her brows, and a glint of concern appeared in her blue eyes.

"Often I am called out in the night to see someone who is dying. You know I preach from an outline. Writing out my sermons for publication takes hours."

She nodded, since she often sat with him while he put his sermons to paper.

"My constant travels will separate us. My ministry often encroaches on my free time. In the light of all of these things—do you still wish to marry me?"

She felt as if ice water had been thrown into her face. Her cheeks froze, and her throat tightened. Taking a deep breath, she tried to find her voice. "Are you saying that...you would rather *not* m-marry me?"

His bushy eyebrows descended, and his mouth crumpled into a frown. "No! No! If I lost you, my heart would break and bring me close to death. However, I must be sure you understand—the disadvantages."

*Now he is repeating Mama's warnings. Do I want to marry someone who will be preoccupied—even obsessed—with ministry? He will have less time with me than I might like.* With clenched fists, she imagined refusing his hand. She saw an image of him with tears rolling down his already fatigued face, and a tingle of remorse ran down her spine.

Gritting her teeth, she pushed the picture away. *That would hurt him. I cannot be that selfish. But can I truly accept all the hardship he describes?*

She looked up into his pleading eyes and felt her heart skip a beat. *I love this dear man! In spite of all the disadvantages and adversity, I must marry him.*

Susannah threw her arms around him, while tears ran down her face. "I could not...live without you."

"Oh, S-Susie, my beloved!" he said, his arms around her. He rested his cheek on the top of her head.

She pressed her face against the fabric of his coat, which muffled her reply. "Charles, I love you."

For several minutes, the couple continued to embrace and to repeat vows of unending love. Both forgot Mrs. Thompson's presence.

"Excuse me, Charles, would you like a cup of tea?" Mrs. Thompson stood in front of the couch. She pointed to a silver tea tray that sat on a mahogany chest to their left. "The maid arrived with the tea I ordered."

As Susannah pulled away, she felt a warm blush spread over her face.

Even though he cleared his throat, Charles' voice still had a husky tone when he answered, "Yes, Madam, thank you."

"Sugar and milk?" She raised her eyebrows as she selected a fine china cup from the tray.

He straightened his coat and bowtie. "I prefer milk and two lumps of sugar, please. Thank you."

Mrs. Thompson handed him tea and then turned to her daughter. "Susie, would you also like tea?"

"Yes, thank you, Mama!" Susie sighed. Her body felt limp with all the tension gone.

"Here, my dear," Mrs. Thompson said as she handed the tea to her daughter, "You have chosen to marry a fine man. I know he will not fail you when he escorts you to another service."

"Oh, I forgot!" Spurgeon frowned. He looked around for a place to set his cup.

Susie saw the look in his eye and pointed to the tea tray.

He deposited his cup on the tray and reached inside his coat pocket. "I received a letter from the queen, and she asked me to speak at Windsor. I hoped you would accompany me, Susie."

Lights danced in her eyes as she set her cup aside and accepted the expensive paper he handed her. "You mean Windsor *Castle.* They asked you to speak at Windsor?"

"Yes, I shall preach to the queen and her household." A smile lit up his brown eyes.

"This is an incredible honor," Susie said, gazing at the fine parchment bearing the queen's signature. For a moment she held the invitation to her heart, feeling breathless. "I would be *delighted* to accompany you."

"I am thrilled for you, Charles. May I see the invitation?" Mrs. Thompson asked. She now sat in the French chair, holding her own teacup. Susie handed her mother the paper, which she read and then returned to Spurgeon.

As he placed it back in his pocket, he said, "Dearest, I shall strive to keep you in mind—even before my sermon. I prefer not to repeat the same mistake."

She took a sip of tea, and as the warmth spread over her body, she smiled at him. "If I slip from your thoughts, I shall not forget the man I love has a special anointing of God. Instead of losing my temper, I shall inform the queen that I am learning to be patient with my absent-minded fiancé."

A mischievous smile danced on his face, "And I shall humbly brag on your forbearance while God makes me into a better man."

The three chatted about the visit to Windsor as they drank their tea. Afterward, Susie accompanied Spurgeon to the entrance hall. Standing on a thick floral rug surrounded by palms, they said their farewells.

"Goodbye, beloved." Spurgeon ran his finger along her cheek, tilted her face toward his, and planted a gentle kiss on her mouth.

His lips released hers, and she gazed up into his brown eyes. "Goodbye!"

He turned, went out the door, and descended her front steps while holding the ornate iron railings.

She walked back to the sitting room and pulled aside the curtains to gaze into the fog which often enfolded London. The gas lanterns by the road shed a soft, fuzzy light onto the cobblestone street in front of her house, but in the darkness, she could no longer see Spurgeon. Tears gathered in her eyes. *Thank you for this man! He is truly a gift from heaven. What other man would have apologized so humbly? Today you taught me a vital lesson—one a pastor's wife must know. After we marry, I could keep him from ministry by demanding his time. Instead, I shall release him to you for service. Thank you for allowing me to share his life and love.*

# APPENDIX 1

# Epilogue

Chapter 1: Royal Crisis

During Tudor times, spelling wasn't standard. Susan James made special note of the way the queen spelled her own name—Kateryn.[1] The queen's tomb at Sudeley Castle also bears the same spelling.

With the king's approval, Kateryn published a book of poems in 1545. The king died in January of 1547, and she remarried soon afterward. Later that year, she published a confession of faith, *Lamentations of a Sinner*. In 1548, she gave birth to a daughter but died of infection a few days later.

Chapter 2: The Price of Freedom

Louise died of uterine cancer five years after she remarried. Research shows human papilloma virus (HPV) can cause uterine cancer. Promiscuous men often contract the disease. While men show no symptoms, they can pass the disease on to their spouses.[2] The duke had contact with prostitutes as well as young girls and could have been infected

---

[1] James, Susan, *Kateryn Parr: the making of a queen,* 1999

[2] www.cancer.gov/cancertopics/factsheet/Risk/HPV

with HPV. If Louise caught HPV from her husband, it would explain her early death.

Louise's older son became Duke Ernest II of Saxe-Coburg-Gotha. Her younger son, Albert, married Queen Victoria who gave him the title Prince Consort.

Chapter 3: Contagious!

Katie Luther operated a boarding house and several farms. Her keen mind and good business sense made her husband a wealthy man. Their home provided a wonderful outlet for ministry. After supper her husband talked to the students for hours. Years after his death, students printed their conversations—*Table Talk.*

Chapter 4: The Journey

After Frittie died, Alice broke all ties with Strauss. She told her lady-in-waiting that she had new insight into Christianity and spoke warmly of loved ones in heaven. Despite fragile health, she helped widows find employment, supported hospitals, and championed the education of nurses. At 38, in 1878, she died of diphtheria on the anniversary of her father's death, December 14.

Chapter 5: Whispers

During her life, Caroline Bauer published two books about her theatrical career, but she made no reference to her short marriage. After she died, her friends published the story of her marriage. In 1887, an admirer translated her story from German into English and printed it in London.

Chapter 6: A Handful of Peppermint Candy

Ellen McCallie had twelve children, but only six lived to adulthood. Despite her large family, Ellen participated in many community activities. Her home was always open to a traveling minister or a needy person.

Two of her sons started McCallie School for boys in Chattanooga. Her daughter, Grace McCallie, co-founded Girls' Preparatory School.

Chapter 7: A Figure of Wax

Emperor Frederick III ruled Prussia for ninety days. After his death, Vicky bought a home outside Frankfurt and retired there. She collected fine paintings and kept up family ties until her death in 1901.

Chapter 8: Starting Over

Katie Luther maintained her boarding house until 1552, when plague forced university officials to relocate the school in Torgau. She fled the city with her two youngest children. While staying in Torgau, she died at the age of 53.

Chapter 9: Frenzied Flight

Catherine and Bertie moved from place to place in Europe until Mary died. When Protestant Elizabeth ascended to the throne, the family returned. Elizabeth I didn't reform the English church as extensively as Catherine had hoped. The duchess believed the elaborate ceremonies distracted people from the simplicity of the gospel.

Chapter 10: A Better Man

Susannah and Spurgeon married in 1856. She gave birth to twin boys, Thomas and Charles. Illness kept her from an active life, yet she maintained a fund which gave books, clothing, and stationery to needy ministers.

# APPENDIX 2

# Questions for Thought and Discussion

Chapter 1: Royal Crisis

1. What does Matthew 5:10–12 have to say about Kateryn's problem?
2. Kateryn didn't want to marry the king. What can we learn from Esther 4:14 about her position in England during the Reformation?
3. When Kateryn learned she angered Henry VIII, she feared he would behead her as he had two of his other wives. Read 1 Corinthians 15:55–57. Compare and contrast a believer's view of death with a nonbeliever's view of death.
4. While queen, Kateryn had Bible studies and taught her maids to read. Educating women was a new idea. Read 2 Timothy 2:15, Romans 12:2, and Ezra 7:10. Discuss why education is a biblical idea.
5. Read 1 Samuel 25:2–38. Compare Abigail and Kateryn. What can you learn from these two ladies about how a wife should submit to her husband?

6. Before Kateryn went to apologize to the king, she bathed in herbs and dressed in attractive clothes. Read Matthew 5:28 and 1 Corinthians 7:1–5 and discuss how a woman's appearance impacts her husband. If you are a married woman, what actions will you take based on what you learned?

Chapter 2: The Price of Freedom

1. Do you agree with the way Louise chose to get freedom? Did she like the outcome of her choice? What steps should we take when making a decision? See Proverbs 1:5b and Proverbs 15:22.
2. In the Old Testament, God reveals how he hates injustice. Read Proverbs 29:7, Isaiah 10:2, Ephesians 5:25, and 1 Peter 3:7, and compare these to the duke's behavior.
3. Read Malachi 2:13–16 and discuss how God deals with men who oppress their wives.
4. Over the years Christians have argued about the role of divorce. Read Matthew 19:8 and Romans 7:2. What is God's ideal for marriage? Discuss the effects of sin. Read Romans 6:23.
5. In Louise's day, a wife needed to maintain pristine morals, while her husband could do whatever he pleased. Contrast this attitude with 2 Chronicles 19:7 and Galatians 2:6.
6. The duchess and von Hanstein fell in love even though they maintained moral purity. Why do you think Scripture gave the commands in 1 Corinthians 7:1–2?
7. Read Psalm 9:9 and Proverbs 21:1. Discuss why the King of Prussia gave von Hanstein a title.

Chapter 3: Contagious!

1. Read Philippians 4:6 and discuss how Katie handled her fear. What advice could you give her about handling her fear?

2. Today the death of a child often splits up a marriage. How could Dr. Luther put his wife and unborn child at risk after losing an infant? See 2 Samuel 12:22–23 and Romans 1:14–17.
3. Katie disagreed with her husband about caring for someone who might have the plague. What should a wife do when she disagrees with her husband? See Ephesians 5:22 and Daniel 1:8.
4. Read Ephesians 5:25–28. Who does God hold accountable for the success of the family? How does this explain God's command for a wife to submit to her husband?
5. Are there limits to authority, or do we always have to obey? Acts 5:29, Exodus 1:15–21.
6. Like the Luther family, other Christians have cared for people who are ill—even at risk to their own health. What is the origin of those values? See Philippians 2:3–8, Matthew 10:28, Hebrews 11:17–19, 1 John 3:17.

Chapter 4: The Journey

1. Alice lived a life full of sorrow and, as a result, feared the future. Describe a Christian view of death. See John 11:25–26 and 1 Corinthians 15:55–57.
2. Why didn't Alice like the comfort Strauss offered?
3. Should believers grieve the loss of a loved one or *just* praise God? If so, then how should believers grieve? 1 Thessalonians 4:13–14.
4. Alice questioned her faith and wanted answers. Compare what she did to the Berean church in Acts 17:10–11. Read Acts 17:17, Acts 18:4, Acts 19:8–9. Could Paul have reasoned if Christianity was ridiculous?
5. Is there enough proof to validate our faith, or do we have blind faith? See 1 Corinthians 15, and look very closely at verse 6. How likely is it that 500 people would see something that didn't exist?

6. What is faith? See Hebrews 11:1–3. Can you *prove* the existence of God, or must you live by faith? Romans 1:17.
7. What is the sign of the resurrection? Did Jesus fulfill this sign? See Matthew 12:39–40 and Romans 1:3–4.
8. Was Alice a true believer? See Philippians 1:6.
9. How did faith change Alice's perspective? See Hebrews 11, especially verse 32 to the end of the chapter.

Chapter 5: Whispers

1. What did Caroline want?
2. What do you want? Where should you get your needs met? John 7:37–38.
3. Compare Leopold's idea of marriage and Romans 7:2.
4. Should a man think of his wife as a disposable object? See 1 Peter 3:7.
5. Why did Leopold marry? Did he consider the needs and concerns of his wife? See Philippians 2.
6. How does following the commands of Christ impact the husband and wife relationship? How does it impact friendship? See Exodus 20:12–17, Galatians 5:14, and Galatians 5:22–23.
7. Caroline and her mother trusted Baron Stockmar. Later they wished they hadn't. Why should you be careful whom you trust? Read Isaiah 53:6 and Romans 3.
8. What criteria should we consider before we trust someone? See 1 Timothy 5:22. Elders are ordained by the laying on of hands. What does this verse teach about ordaining someone we hardly know?
9. How did Caroline attempt to get Leopold's attention? What other actions could she have taken? Matthew 18:15–17, Romans 12:18, Romans 13:8.

Chapter 6: A Handful of Peppermint Candy

1. Rev. McCallie stayed in Chattanooga during the war and put his family in danger. Compare Matthew 4:5–7 and Luke 14:26. Decide under what conditions it is okay to put your life and the lives of your family in danger to serve God.
2. Ellen struggled with her husband's decision. She wanted him to minister in a safer place. In your own life, how much effort should you exert to fulfill the Great Commission as a disciple of Christ? Compare Mark 8:34 and 2 Samuel 24:22–24.
3. Read Psalm 139:17–18 and Matthew 23:37. Compare and contrast God's love for Ellen's baby and Ellen's love for her baby.
4. Compare Romans 8:18 with Ellen's anxiety about the war.
5. Read Habakkuk 3:16–19, and compare verse 16 and verse 19. Does living by faith mean we *don't* have feelings?
6. What could Ellen have learned about God from reading Philippians 4:10–13?
7. Read Ephesians 5:25. If you have read *Whispers*, compare how Leopold dealt with his wife to how McCallie handled his wife. Which one comes closest to the example of Christ?
8. Rev. McCallie was horrified by the sight of the severed arms and legs that surgeons had thrown into the yard after the battle. Read Romans 6:23 and Galatians 5:19–21, then discuss how sin impacts our world.

Chapter 7: A Figure of Wax

1. What two things did Vicky want?
2. Discuss whether it is easy or difficult to find peace in this world. See Romans 8:20–23.
3. Where did Vicky search for peace and strength to sustain her in tough times? How does this compare to 1 Corinthians 2:1–2?
4. Compare Vicky's faith in science with Matthew 7:24–27.

5. Describe Vicky's relationship with Wilhelm and compare it to Exodus 20:12.
6. How did Vicky redefine the resurrection? How do nonbelievers handle the death of a loved one today?
7. What does God say about the resurrection? See Luke 24:38–43, 1 Corinthians 15:17–23.
8. How did Vicky find peace at the end of the story? Compare this to 2 Corinthians 1:7, Hebrews 6:17–19, and 1 Peter 1:3.

Chapter 8: Starting Over

1. Many feminists in our day believe the Bible oppresses women. Read Proverbs 31:16–18 and discuss God's view of women.
2. After Luther married, Katie created an atmosphere in which he could impact many lives for Christ. After his death, students published parts of his conversations around the supper table—*Table Talk*. Compare Katie's actions to Proverbs 31:23–25.
3. How can you create an atmosphere in your home to impact lives for Christ?
4. Katie had a great deal of respect for her husband and called him Dr. Luther. Read Ephesians 5:33 and Proverbs 31:23. Discuss the importance of respect in the husband and wife relationship.
5. In Katie's day women couldn't own a business or buy and sell. With her husband's signature, she carried out business and even made her husband wealthy. Compare Proverbs 31:11–12 to the ideas of Katie's time.
6. Read Proverbs 14:1 and discuss how Katie obeyed this command. What steps can you take to obey this command today?
7. Drinking beer is a German tradition, and Katie earned money selling beer in the town square. Alcoholics, however, must avoid alcohol altogether. Read 1 Corinthians 8:1–13 and discuss how to avoid causing an alcoholic to stumble.

Chapter 9: Frenzied Flight

1. When Queen Mary came to the throne, she imprisoned and executed ministers who preached the gospel. Compare her actions to Romans 1:18 and Luke 8:12.
2. Read Numbers 14:18 and discuss how Henry VIII's sin impacted his daughter's life.
3. At that time, Protestants feared the oppression of the pope. Read Proverbs 31:9 and Jeremiah 5:28. Discuss how we can prevent oppression today.
4. Read Matthew 5:44 and compare it to Catherine, who chose to name her dog after someone she disliked.
5. Contrast Catholic views of marriage and Protestant views of marriage at that time. What incorrect ideas does our generation hold about marriage?
6. Read the story of Rahab in Joshua 2 and compare it to Hebrews 11:31 and James 2:25. Discuss the use of deceit in Catherine and Bertie's escape.

Chapter 10: A Better Man

1. Spurgeon violated a rule in Victorian society. His actions hurt Susannah, because he didn't treat her with respect. Read 1 Peter 2:17. Discuss whether or not Susannah should have expected to be treated with respect.
2. Read Matthew 18:15–17 and Ephesians 4:15 and discuss what to do if someone offends us.
3. Read James 1:15 and discuss why it is hard to talk to someone who has offended you.
4. Compare Spurgeon's apology to Genesis 3:9–13. Do you agree or disagree with what he did? Why?

5. Read 1 Peter 4:8. In this verse, the word *cover* means "hide." How does this verse apply to Susannah and Mrs. Thompson? Should Mrs. Thompson have offered Spurgeon an excuse?
6. Review Ephesians 4:15 and discuss how this experience might have prepared Susannah for marriage.
7. Read 1 Corinthians 13:4 and discuss how Susannah could obey this verse as the wife of a busy pastor.
8. How did Susannah and Spurgeon grow as a result of this situation?

# References

Alice, Helena August Victoria, and Karl Sell. 1884. *Alice grand duchess of Hesse, princess of Great Britain and Ireland, biographical sketch and letters.* London: J. Murray.

Bauer, Karoline. 1887. *Caroline Bauer and the Coburgs.* London: Vizetelly & Co.

Cooper, Eleanor. 1982. *Don't Say "You," Say "We": the founding of Girls Preparatory School 1906–1918.* Chattanooga: Bruiser Press.

Foxe, John, and M. Hobart Seymour. 1855. *The acts and monuments of the church containing the history and sufferings of the martyrs: wherein is set forth at large the whole race and course of the church, from the primitive age to these later times, with a preliminary dissertation on the difference between the church of Rome that now is and the ancient church of Rome that then was.* New York: R. Carter.

James, Susan E. 1999. *Kateryn Parr the making of a queen.* Women and gender in early modern England, 1500–1750. Aldershot, Hants: Ashgate.

Luther, Martin. *The Complete Works of Martin Luther.* My Fortress Press/ Concordia Publishing House Products. CD Rom.

Martin, Theodore. 1880. *The life of His Royal Highness the Prince consort, vol. five.* London: Smith, Elder, & Co.

Macdonnell, Anne Lumb. 1913. *Reminiscences of diplomatic life; being stray memories of personalities and incidents connected with several European courts and also with life in South America fifty years ago.* London: A. & C. Black.

McCallie, Thomas Hooke, Katherine McCallie Johnson, and James Park McCallie. 1959. *An early family record of the McCallie family in Tennessee: an autobiographical sketch and genealogy of his family.* s.l : s.n.

National Cancer Institute. www.cancer.gov/cancertopics/factsheet/Risk/ HPV, (access date November 29, 2007).

Noel, Gerard. 1974. *Princess Alice Queen Victoria's forgotten daughter.* London: Constable.

Ponsonby, D. A.1958. *The lost Duchess; the story of the Prince consort's mother.* London: Chapman & Hall.

Read, Evelyn. 1963. *My Lady Suffolk, a portrait of Catherine Willoughby, Duchess of Suffolk.* New York: Knopf.

Spurgeon, C.H., Susannah Spurgeon, and W.J. Harrald. 1962. *C. H. Spurgeon, the early years, 1834–1859.* London: Banner of Truth Trust.

Treu, Martin. 2003. *Katherine von Bora Luther's Wife.* Wittenberg: Drei Kantanien Verlag.

Victoria, and Frederick Edward Grey Ponsonby. 1929. *Letters of the Empress Frederick.* London: Macmillian and Co.